WILMETTE PUBLIC LIBRARY

3 1239 00497 0007

P9-DEC-639

X

WITHDRAWN
Wilmette Public Library

Wilmette Public Library
Wilmette, Illinois
Telephone: 256-5025

GAYLORD M

Song of the Sea

Myths, Tales, and Folklore

Ann Spencer

Illustrated by Mark Lang

Tundra Books

WILMETTE PUBLIC LIBRARY

Text copyright © 2001 by Ann Spencer
Illustrations copyright © 2001 by Mark Lang

Published in Canada by Tundra Books, *McClelland & Stewart Young Readers*,
481 University Avenue, Toronto, Ontario M5G 2E9

Published in the United States by Tundra Books of Northern New York,
P.O. Box 1030, Plattsburgh, New York 12901

Library of Congress Control Number: 00-135463

All rights reserved. The use of any part of this publication reproduced, transmitted in
any form or by any means, electronic, mechanical, photocopying, recording, or other-
wise, or stored in a retrieval system, without the prior written consent of the publisher
– or, in case of photocopying or other reprographic copying, a licence from the
Canadian Copyright Licensing Agency – is an infringement of the copyright law.

Canadian Cataloguing in Publication Data

Spencer, Ann, 1955-
    Song of the sea : myths, tales, and folklore

ISBN 0-88776-487-8

1. Ocean – Folklore.   2. Sea stories.   I. Lang, Mark.   II. Title.

PS8587.P317S66 2001   J398.23'2162   C00-932284-1
PZ8.1.S66So 2001

Ann Spencer gratefully acknowledges the support of the Canada Council for the Arts
in assisting her with this project.

We acknowledge the support of the Canada Council for the Arts and the Ontario Arts
Council for our publishing program.

ONTARIO ARTS COUNCIL
CONSEIL DES ARTS DE L'ONTARIO

We acknowledge the financial support of the Government of Canada through the
Book Publishing Industry Development Program for our publishing activities.

The lines from "maggie and milly and molly and may." Copyright © 1956, 1984,
1991 by the Trustees for the E. E. Cummings Trust, from COMPLETE POEMS:
1904–1962 by E. E. Cummings, edited by George J. Firmage. Used by permission of
Liveright Publishing Corporation.

Although folktales and folk songs are by their very nature oral traditions, every
reasonable effort has been made to locate and acknowledge the owners of copyright
material in this volume. Any information about errors or omissions would be
welcomed by the publisher.

Design: Ingrid Paulson

Printed and bound in Canada

1 2 3 4 5 6   06 05 04 03 02 01

For my grandmother, Jennie Mason, with wonderful memories of foggy Lunenburg nights spent around Nannie's kitchen table: her freshly baked rolls warmed us and her stories of forerunners, shipwrecks, and life along the seashores fed our imaginations.

A.S.

For Nathan, Tony, Brendan, Sophie, Zoe, Alexandra, Robin, and Gabriel.

M.L.

Acknowledgments

Thank you to Lynn-Marie Richard at the Maritime Museum of the Atlantic; and to Lee Heald and Laura Pereira at the Old Dartmouth Historical Society – New Bedford Whaling Museum for answering all my nautical questions. Oceans of thanks to my editor, Sue Tate, for her diligence and enthusiasm.

A.S.

J398.2
SPencer

CONTENTS

may came home with a smooth round stone
as small as a world and as large as alone.

For whatever we lose (like a you or a me)
it's always ourselves we find in the sea

– From "maggie and milly and molly and may"
   by E.E. Cummings

I

ANCIENT VOICES: SOUNDING THE CONCH

SOUNDING THE CONCH

Triton rises from the ocean
in his chariot pulled by white surf steeds.
Riding on the crests of waves,
galloping hooves turn blue sea to frothy foam.

Son of Poseidon, god of the ocean,
raise your seashell trumpet.
Sound the conch and play
the most ancient song of the sea.

It is said, it sings: This is how the sea began:
A box there once was, with all the waters of the earth
    shut up tight inside
until the lid was opened by curious hands and the sea
    burst forth.

A great octopus spilled his ink and that was the sea.
The great gods thought up the sea and there it was.

A low, dull blare mingled with pounding surf,
the first song the sea ever sang,
carried over waters, echoing and pulsing
wherever its tones found shore.

Sound the conch, Triton,
so all who hear may know
the song of the great ocean –
gentle and lulling; harsh and tempestuous.
Always deep with mysteries.
An eternal and forever song.

SALMON WOMAN,
THE MAIDEN OF DECEPTION PASS

A narrow channel, marked by swift currents and whirlpools, was the only passage to the sea for the Samish tribe living along Canada's west coast. For a people who depended on the sea for their dietary staples of salmon and shellfish, navigating such dangerous waters was a necessary part of everyday living. But long ago a mysterious incident happened along that western shore that gave the Samish tribe a protector and guide through the pass.

Since then, a sea-maiden has appeared in times of distress, surfacing through whirling waters to lift canoes out of tidal pulls and currents that threaten to drag them straight into the mouth of a whirlpool. Some call her Salmon Woman, but many know her as the Maiden of Deception Pass, where this perilous stretch of seawater is found. The sea-maiden came from the tribe and her story is one of great sacrifice.

ONE SUMMER AFTERNOON, A GROUP OF Samish maidens met at the shore. The tide was low and perfect for digging clams. They talked and laughed softly as they filled their baskets. One young woman was looking out to the waters. She was of a gentle nature and her thoughts were of how beautiful the sea was. A friend, noticing that the maiden had gathered few clams, tossed a big clamshell her way. The shell soared over the girl's head, landing just beyond her in the water. Startled from her peaceful daydream, the young woman waded into the sea to find the clamshell. There it was on the rocky bottom, and she reached in for it. She could feel it in her hand, but when she lifted it out of the water it shot once more into the air, landing farther out in the sea. The girl waded out to just above her knees and bent down to get the clam. Again it slipped away from her hold.

This strangeness continued until the girl found herself in water that now came up to her waist. Keeping her head above the surface, she dipped her whole body straight down into the sea and felt about on the bottom with her hands. She could not find the clamshell amongst all the pebbles and stones.

All of a sudden a hand clutched her own. She gasped and tried to pull free, but to no avail. The girl was so shocked that she could not find the power to scream. And in that stillness, a voice seemed to float upward through the water. "Gentle maid," it said, in a tone like the lapping waves, "I beg you not to be alarmed, for I wish only to behold such great earthly beauty."

At that, the force let go of her hand and her ears were filled with splashing, lapping waves, and the distant laughter of her friends onshore. The girl wondered if she had not gotten caught up in another daydream. Onshore with the others, she spoke not of what had happened.

Again, the next day, the girl met with the maidens to dig for clams. This time, when she looked out to sea, she saw a dancing light sparkling on the waters. "How beautiful it glimmers," she thought, as she walked toward it. It had looked to be so near, but when she reached to put her hand through the glistening ball of light, it appeared to jump just a little ahead of her. As she had done with the clamshell, the girl waded out farther and farther until she found herself standing once again in waist-high waters. This time, when she plunged her hand in to catch the dazzling glow, she was grasped yet again by the hand.

The girl felt no panic. The voice lulled her with its soft sea whispers, telling her stories of a glistening peaceful world beneath the waters. It spoke of many splendors that filled the ocean kingdom – splendors no human could ever imagine. Even the girl, with her vivid daydreams of the beautiful sea, could not envision such beauty. "Come back again," the soothing voice hissed, as the hand let go of hers. Once again, she headed back to her friends, telling no one of the magical happenings.

Day after day, the girl was mysteriously drawn into the water by some sea force. A sound or a wave or a floating object would be there, just beyond her reach. And each time, she was grasped by the hand and told more secrets of the deep. For longer periods each day, she was held in this sea trance.

Then one morning, the girl ventured to the shore alone. This time when she waded out and the hand held on to hers, the waters all about her started to quiver. A handsome young man rose out of the stirred-up sea. "I wish to marry you," he said, "for you are gentle and beautiful, and you alone can understand the ways of my world."

"But my father will never allow such a thing to happen," cautioned the girl, realizing her disappointment in this truth. Yet the sea man was insistent, and the two went into the village to meet with her father. As she had anticipated, they were met with a firm no. The sea man told the father all he had told the maiden. He painted the great beauty of his world with words that moved the girl to tears. But such words had no effect on the father and his decision remained unchanged.

At that, the sea man gave a stern warning. He spoke to the father in a voice that sounded like a crashing wave: "I warn you, old man. If you do not change your mind, your people will suffer greatly, for as well as I know the sea's beauty, I know her dark mysteries. Heed not my words and I shall keep all sea creatures from your reach. Your village will go hungry." With that, he was gone.

At first, small changes were noticed. The girl and her friends came home with half-empty baskets after a full day at the shore. Small streams began to dry up and no salmon ran. Not even shellfish could be found. Where there had been plenty, there was not a fish to be seen.

With the scarcity came sickness and death. The girl knew she must save her village. She ran to the shore and waded out to the spot where the sea man had been. Up to her waist in the water, she cried out, "I beg you, good sea man, return food to my people, for many are dying."

"No," came the voice, sounding like the angry sea itself. "Your father must let us marry. Only then shall there be food." The girl was not frightened by his sternness, but slowly she walked to the shore for she knew the sea man's word was final. There was only one action to take. She must convince her father to let her go for her people's sake.

Finally, as even the freshwater streams were drying out from the great drought of that summer, her father agreed there was no other choice. Not to allow his daughter to marry the man of the sea meant death from starvation for each and every one of his people. He took his daughter's hand and together they walked to the shore and waded out in the salt water to talk to the sea man. When he surfaced, the father spoke. Tears welled in the father's eyes as he gave his permission: "Yes, my daughter may marry you. But I beg you one request be granted me. Allow us the joy of seeing her once a year. I must know she is being treated well under the sea and that she is truly happy. Only then can I let her go in my heart."

The agreement was made and the father turned for shore. When he looked out to the spot, he saw his beautiful daughter take the hand of the young man and together they sank below the gentle waves. His last image of his daughter was of her beautiful raven hair floating all about the surface of the sea.

The father arrived back in his village to find great excitement and relief. Waters spilled to overflowing in all the streams. Salmon leaped and clams squirted. All was well with his people. The man thought of his daughter's great sacrifice and his heart ached.

At the end of one year, he went to the shore and sat looking to the spot in the sea where he had last seen his daughter. He worried that her husband would not allow her to come back to land, but there, in the water, he saw something floating. At first he thought it was only a tangle of seaweed, but then he remembered his daughter's raven hair. The sea stirred and his daughter appeared in the waist-high water. She walked to her father and together they went to the village.

Great was the thanks expressed to her. All asked if she was happy and she told them stories of her beautiful sea home. One night, her father noticed her at the doorway looking out to the ocean. She seemed to be listening intently to something his ears could not hear. He let her alone with her world. The next morning he walked her back to the shore. She hardly heard his good-byes for she waded quickly through the waters and once more disappeared beneath the surface.

For three more years she returned to the village. Her people rejoiced, for her visits were marked with good fortune in their fishing. But her father saw greater changes in his daughter with each year's passing. Where at first she had looked out to sea only in the evening, now she was always casting her eyes toward the water. She became impatient and distracted when folk tried to speak to her. It was as if some great part of herself was missing.

Her appearance was changing too. Early on, a friend noticed that her hair had a greenish glow; in fact, in certain lights, all of her skin looked bluish green. Her girlfriends thought it was the play of late-summer light, but on the third visit there was no mistaking that she was indeed changing. When her father clasped her hands, he was alarmed at how rough they felt. He held them up to kiss and tried not to gasp aloud at the sight of small barnacles growing on her knuckles and wrists. A friend spied the same spread of barnacles on her bare feet. By the end of that visit, many saw that the barnacles were growing up her arms and legs.

By the fourth summer, the barnacles covered her face on one side, from her chin to her temple. Green seagrass grew wildly in her raven hair and cold breezes followed her about on her walks through the village, and even when she was indoors. All about her was a deep sadness and longing. She looked out to sea with her sand-encrusted eyes – everyone knew she yearned to return.

Her father realized the sea was now her true home. He looked one last time at his daughter, the sea-maiden, then gave her his blessing to go back to the water. "You need not continue coming to land," he said, "unless you desire to." She wept salty tears and ran to the shore. With one splash she was gone.

Although the girl came no more to land, she never forgot her love for her people. Salmon Woman, the Maiden of Deception Pass, would always act as their protector. She cared for and guided those lost or in danger in the channel. She provided them with streams full of salmon and seas laden with shellfish. Always she was with them, guarding and guiding. The Samish people had only to look out to sea, where her greenish raven hair floated on the surface, to know they would always be protected by their beautiful sea-maiden. In even the swiftest of currents or rushing tidal waters, they knew Salmon Woman would appear, wading through the channel to guide them safely to shore.

PRAYER FOR SMOOTH WATERS

Ocean Spirit
calm the waves for me
get close to me, my power
my heart is tired
make the sea like milk for me
yeho
yehólo

– Traditional Haida prayer

TIEN-HOU,
THE SAILOR GODDESS

On the small island of Mei-chou, just off the coast of China, a mystical story is still told of a young girl who became the sailor goddess. Boats and junks travelling over the seas around her island almost always carry her image aboard. Sailors, traders, and passengers all ask Tien-Hou for divine protection.

TIEN-HOU HAD NOT ALWAYS BEEN A GODDESS. She started out in life normally as a little girl living on an island with her parents and her four older brothers. The family made their living from the sea. While her father and brothers were out fishing, Tien-Hou stayed on the island with her mother. They worked with the other women, weaving baskets and gathering beach shells, then traded their creations for dyed fabrics and pottery jugs.

Tien-Hou did not mind weaving, for as her hands worked the familiar patterns, her mind was free to roam. She stared longingly across the turquoise-blue seas beyond the white sands. How she wished she could go out on the water like the men of her family. But her wishes were mixed with worries for the safety of her father and brothers out at sea as they could not swim.

One warm and sunny day, Tien-Hou was sitting on the beach under a shady palm tree with her mother. From time to time the young girl squinted across the water to the horizon, hoping the men's boat would soon come into sight. For hours Tien-Hou had absentmindedly woven her baskets and daydreams to the sleepy rhythms of the lapping waves. All of a sudden, her head felt as if it might explode. Her body shuddered, then stiffened, and her eyes rolled back in her head. Rigid and gasping for breath, Tien-Hou fell over in the sand.

Her mother was greatly distressed. She shook the girl to wake her up, then cradled the small fevered body in her arms. There were no convulsions, but Tien-Hou's breathing was raspy and erratic. Her mother cried out and other women from the island came quickly to help carry Tien-Hou back to her family's hut. There, they spread her out on a bamboo mat. Throughout that long afternoon, the kind mother dipped cloths in cold water and placed them on Tien-Hou's brow. The fever would not break and the girl seemed lost to the world.

Now the mother wept and pleaded to her daughter to break free of the coma's hold. Over and over she whispered to Tien-Hou, "Wake up, wake up, Tien-Hou. It's your mama. Do you hear me? Wake up now, my love."

Tien-Hou began to tremble as she heard the love and worry in her mother's voice. She opened her eyes and stared at her mother. "If only I could have stayed longer; oh, I should have stayed just a moment longer" were the words spoken through her parched lips. Her eyes welled up with tears.

So happy was her mother at Tien-Hou's revival that she thought little of these strange words, sure that they were only fevered mutterings and had no meaning. But that evening when her husband's boat returned to the island, she realized too well the significance of what Tien-Hou had been saying. Something inexplicable had occurred out at sea that day. A savage storm had come up and tossed the little fishing boat around the waters like a top. A giant wave swept the father and the brothers from the deck. Each one thought he was about to drown when he saw Tien-Hou nearing the water. She seemed to fly down from the heavens and lifted them, one at a time, from the turbulent sea safely onto the deck. But at the exact moment when the fourth brother called out for help, Tien-Hou vanished into the misty air. The drowning brother cried out several times from the violent waves, then called out no more. When the sea calmed, the father and the brothers made one last desperate search, then reluctantly headed for shore.

Tien-Hou rose from her mat and spoke clearly and quietly to her family: "That was why I did not wish to be awakened. My job was not complete and I wanted to stay on to save my brother. But the pain in your voice and the love in your heart drew me back to you, Mother." Bringing one child back to life had cost the life of another, and the family was confused and full of grief for a long time.

Tien-Hou's strange state was put out of mind for many months. The mother resolved to forget about it completely until one day, Tien-Hou again fell into a feverish trance. Although her heart ached, the mother knew she must not wake her daughter.

This time Tien-Hou lapsed into a deep coma. For years her body lay still and was tended to by her mother and the village women. Those who washed and cared for her remarked that she seemed not to be in her body at all.

The only consolation to her mother and relatives was that fishing boats landing on the island would tell stories of miracles: how a beautiful young maiden had soared from the sky like a bird to rescue those in peril. She pulled many from raging seas; she held wrecked boats safely together until they made shore; she swept pirate boats away from their unsuspecting targets.

For many years the little body on the bamboo mat was cared for until a time when all life ceased to flow through Tien-Hou. But even with her death, the courageous flying girl's miraculous rescues continued. All along the coastal waters, people still saw her. Now they referred to Tien-Hou, the Sailor Goddess, with great respect as the Queen Protector of the Sea. And since she appeared from the skies, they also called her the Empress of Heaven.

Sailors placed shrines on the left side of the bow on junks and boats travelling those seas. With deep gratitude for her help and guidance, they knelt before statues and images of Tien-Hou. They burned incense morning and evening in her honor, and hung red bags filled with the fragrant ashes around the junk. When storms arose they called out to her for safe passage.

The image of Tien-Hou is of a girl with her neck outstretched like a bird's and her hand cupped over her ear to hear distant sounds of distress, or sheltering her eyes to peer out over the waters to search for those in danger. She is thought to see and hear all with her "thousand-mile eye" and "favorable-mind ear." Some say Tien-Hou can still be seen riding across the sky on clouds, as she protects all those who travel the waters off the coast of China.

SEDNA, THE GREAT WOMAN OF THE SEA

Long ago in the Far North, in the mysterious "way-back time" of ancestors and spirits, there lived a beautiful pigtailed maiden named Sedna. She and her father lived beside the harsh and icy Arctic Ocean in a tent made of animal skins. Sedna had an uncommon beauty made all the more rare by her spirited nature. She was graceful, proud, and wildly free. Her father thought his daughter fickle and haughty, for although young men from across the North had come as suitors, Sedna refused them all.

SEDNA'S GREATEST JOY CAME FROM HER LONG walks along the rugged coastline. One warm day after such a walk, she sat on a large rock and stared far out to sea. Her eyes fixed on the bright rays of the sun, darting and flickering on the pieces of ice floating by. The dance of colors was mesmerizing until the ice prism was shattered by the blade of a paddle rippling through the water. Sedna looked up to see a stranger seated in a kayak, making his way toward the shore. He appeared to be most handsome and wore a splendid parka of rich caribou with wolverine trim. He carried an ivory spear, which gleamed in the sunlight.

As she strained to get a better look at him, Sedna became aware of the sound of birds. It seemed to drift in softly at first, but all of sudden the air was alive with their piercing cries. Birds circled near her, just overhead, until she felt dizzy and faint. Then, in the loud and insistent cawing, one bird voice stood out from the rest. Although she could not be sure exactly when it happened, at some point on that warm afternoon Sedna realized she could understand the meaning of that birdcall. It was as if she was hearing actual words spoken, or perhaps sung. Then she looked out to the mysterious stranger in the kayak. It was his call rising through the cries. He crooned a wooing ballad, full of promises:

Come with me, Sedna.
We will sail away to a fine land –
A home of luxury beyond your dearest dreams.
There you shall live in the most beautiful of tents
And rest peacefully in a warm bed covered in bearskin.
Choruses of birds will serenade you to sleep
And awaken you at day's light.
Your lamp will forever remain full.
Come with me, Sedna.

Yes, this was the suitor she had been waiting for and Sedna felt drawn to go with him. His song had filled her with a strange comfort, as if she were in a happy dream. Not even the chilly sting of a rising wind could bring her to her senses. Sedna walked to the edge of the shore and got into the kayak.

When her father returned from the day's hunting, he looked for his daughter. Far over the waters, where sea met sky, he saw two figures in a kayak. Behind them followed a flock of petrels. He thought he heard their cries, but the sound was more like jeering laughter.

Sedna and the man journeyed, for many days and nights, over seas she did not recognize. To her, it was a strange, dreamlike world of constant howling wind, splashing lapping waves, and cries of many birds. Now and again, within those sounds, Sedna thought she heard the stranger's voice. Then he pointed and Sedna saw land ahead. When they arrived onshore, the man showed Sedna her new home and they became man and wife.

Once she was inside the tent, Sedna saw luxurious bear pelts, just as had been described. Exhausted, she fell asleep on what appeared to be a bed made of bearskin.

Her husband left early every morning to hunt, bringing back all they needed. To Sedna, one perfect day wove seamlessly into the next, until she felt she had lived there always.

But in the Far North land of "way-back time," the visible world could easily deceive. It was not uncommon for powerful spirits to create illusions that seemed perfectly real.

One morning Sedna awoke and spotted the snow goggles her husband always wore lying at the entrance to the tent. Thinking that he would need to wear them for the day's hunting, she dressed and ran to find him.

As she made her way around a large rock, Sedna saw her husband up ahead. Just as she was about to call out, he stopped on the spot, threw his head back, and stretched his arms to the side. What happened next frightened Sedna. There, in front of her very eyes, her husband was changing his form – shape-shifting magic, she had heard it was called. His arms were now massive wings; his caribou clothing, feathers; his mukluks, wiry snarled feet. In her panic to leave, she kicked some pebbles. Her husband swivelled his head and, as Sedna took cover behind the rock, she caught a quick glimpse of his face. It was twisted and grotesque. His beady eyes glared in her direction. Then, satisfied nothing was there, he took wing and flew out over the water. The illusion was finally shattered and Sedna knew her husband was really a non-human – a bird spirit in the form of a powerful fulmar.

She rushed back to her home only to discover more deception. There was no beautiful tent, just a rocky cliff ledge strewn with feathers and dirty pecked fish skins. With all enchantment lifted,

Sedna was distraught. She faced the open sea, weeping and shouting in grief and anger. The breeze carried her wails toward the shore, where her father now lived alone.

The father thought of his daughter with great sadness, for the coming of the warm winds reminded him that a full year had passed since she had left. As he looked out at the sea, he heard the creaking and cracking of the ice. It was moaning in a way he had never heard before. It sounded like a woman's voice. He thought it an illusion and was about to turn from shore when he recognized his daughter's call: "Father, Father, help me."

The father packed his kayak for the journey and set out to sea, with only his daughter's cries to guide him. Days later he found her, wretched and alone on the desolate shore. Sedna held on tight to her father and begged him to take her home. Her bird husband had left for the day and they could make a fast escape. The father agreed it was the only plan and, despite his exhaustion, they set out on the open sea for the journey home.

At first all was well and they seemed to be leaving the shore unnoticed, except by a small flock of petrels flying high above them. Minutes later, the petrels' cries rang out in the distance. The bird husband heard the call of alarm and flew home to find that his wife had fled. Shaking and squawking, he transformed himself back into his human body and got into the kayak. Propelled by the power of his great rage, the kayak quickly began to catch up to Sedna's boat. The flock flew eerily overhead.

The bird husband stood up in the kayak, shouting out his demands that his wife be returned to him. Sedna's father ignored him and paddled harder. The bird man screamed out words of revenge that turned into wild squawks and screeches. Sedna's father panicked at the sound, but dared to look back. Where there had been a man, there now stood a giant fulmar. Sedna's father held tight to the polar bear charm and eagle beak amulet hanging from his belt. Not even the foxtails and animal skins fastened to the prow of his kayak could charm away the horror of the situation.

With each beat of the fulmar's massive wings, the wind began to pick up and waves slapped against the kayak. They rose to frightening heights and the sky blackened as the gigantic fulmar flew overhead. His shrieks, dives, and darts in the midst of the stormy seas drove Sedna's father to his knees in terror.

The father knew he could not hold out against this powerful bird spirit. It was clear to him that if he did not sacrifice Sedna to appease the angry sea, he too would be lost. His cowardly nature took over and, in the grip of this terror, the father threw his daughter into the icy waters. He thought the plunge would be the end of her, but Sedna was strong and determined. She resurfaced and held fast to the side of the kayak. Her father pried at her fingers, but she would not let go. By now he had lost all reason and grabbed for the nearest object to loosen his daughter's grip and send her into the deep.

He smashed at her hands with an ax and Sedna's fingertips fell into the sea. Immediately they turned into fish. Sedna managed to hold on. Another strike of the ax and her fingers came off to the second joint. When they touched the water, they became seals. Still she clung to the boat and her father wielded his final blow. Off came the tops of her fingers and they transformed into walruses. Sedna slid from the kayak and sank into the icy depths.

But that was not the end of Sedna. Because of her sacrifice and the great sea beasts that had been born from her suffering, she was given supernatural powers. Sedna was transformed from a land maiden to a sea goddess. She became the Great Woman of the Sea.

Sedna reigns from her ocean kingdom at the bottom of the Arctic Ocean. As mother of the sea beasts, she is a benevolent goddess and a great provider to the people on land when her rules are followed. Should a taboo be broken, her retaliation is savage and swift. Sedna raises storms on the sea and brings famine by making all whales and polar bears invisible to hunters, and by hiding the seals in the drip-basin beneath her lamp in her house at the bottom of the sea.

Only the angakok, *a shaman or medicine man who has the knowledge of great spirit mysteries, can bring an end to the sickness, starvation, and misery. In a seer's trance, he descends to the watery realm to soothe the angered Sedna. His is a spirit journey marked with peril as he passes violent ice and underwater spirits who lure the drowned. A boiling cauldron and vicious black dog guard Sedna's domain.*

There sits the sea goddess, her face distorted by sadness, suffering, and fierce rage she feels for the people. Their ingratitude and broken taboos have gathered in Sedna's hair like grease, tangling it. Without her fingers, she cannot clean or braid her long hair. The shaman calmly works out all the knots, combs out the grime, and plaits her long black hair. He massages her aching hands and promises the sea goddess that his people will respect her rules and be mindful of the sacredness of life. Sedna promises to free the beasts and allow them to seek the hunters. With order restored, the shaman journeys back to the world of humans to remind them that the bounty of the ocean is to be drawn from with respect, gratitude, and wisdom.

POSEIDON

DEEP IN THE BLUE WATERS OF THE AEGEAN Sea lived Poseidon, the mighty sea god of Ancient Greece. He reigned from his undersea palace of pearl and coral, attended by his marine court. Seated on a shelled throne, Poseidon listened and weighed matters in the world above. When those earthly affairs needed closer scrutiny, Poseidon and a party from his court left the crystal caves housed in the kingdom and readied the white chariot horses in their underwater stables. Triton sounded the conch, signalling the regal party's rise to the water's surface. Poseidon rode over the waves in a chariot of blue and gold, like sea and sun, drawn by his one hundred shining white surf stallions. Always at his side were dolphins, hippocampi, and all manner of sea creatures.

The supreme ruler of the waves and the watery world beneath held a powerful trident, whose three points could calm the most monstrous of marine beasts, shatter shore rocks, and whip up the seas. When Poseidon was content, the seas were serene. But being wild tempered and moody by nature, the sea god would often raise his trident and roar with his thunderous voice until gigantic waves pounded the shores and floods swept over the land. When horribly vexed, Poseidon caused earthquakes to shake from the seabed, and sent fierce sea monsters to attack ships.

Both sea and shore trembled from the sea god's wrath. To appease their stern sea god, Ancient Greek mariners made mighty and costly offerings. They sacrificed black-and-white bulls and some sailors threw gold rings into the ocean, chanting special verses to win favor on the waters. It was the price of calm seas.

II

BEASTLY WAILS: THE SEA AND ALL THEREIN

SEA MONSTER SIGHTINGS

A very large Sea-Serpent of a length of 200 feet and 20 feet in diameter which lives in rocks and in holes near the shore of Bergen; it comes out of its cavern only on summer nights and in fine weather to destroy calves, lambs, or hogs, or goes into the sea to eat cuttles, lobster, and all kinds of sea crabs. It has a growth of hairs of two feet in length hanging from the neck, sharp scales of a dark brown color, and brilliant flaming eyes.

– *Olaus Magnus (1490–1557)*

The (Sea) Monster was of so huge a Size, that coming out of the Water its Head reached as high as the Mast-Head; its Body was as bulky as the Ship, and three or four times as long. It had a long pointed Snout, and spouted like a Whale-Fish; great broad Paws, and the Body seemed covered with shell-work, its skin very rugged and uneven. The under Part of its body was shaped like an enormous huge Serpent, and when it dived again under Water, it plunged backwards into the Sea and so raised its Tail aloft, which seemed a whole Ship's Length distant from the bulkiest part of its Body.

– Danish missionary Hans Egede's account of
a sea monster sighting off Greenland in 1734

I could have sworn the brute's eyes burned at me . . . Then I remember chiefly a dreadful sliminess with a Herculean power behind it . . . something whipped round my left forearm and the back of my neck binding the two together . . . In the same flash, another something slapped itself high on my forehead . . . a mouth began to nuzzle below my throat . . . the suckers felt like hot rings pulling at my skin.

– Account of an attack by a Giant Octopus
by Arthur Grimble, a man who got away

. . . a huge beast which suddenly appeared level with the bulwarks presenting most terrific appearance . . . It seemed covered with large sea shells and to have a big hairy head. Its head could be seen some distance at one side (of the ship) while the tail was still visible many yards away at the other. Its length was estimated to be sixty feet.

– Report sighting off South Africa, by
crewman of the steamship Churchill

JONAH AND THE WHALE

Now the Lord had prepared a great fish to swallow up Jonah. And Jonah was in the belly of the fish three days and three nights.

– Book of Jonah, 1:17

LONG AGO NEAR THE SEA OF GALILEE, THERE lived a man named Jonah. One day he heard the voice of God speaking to him. "Jonah," said God, "the people of the great city of Nineveh have forgotten their goodness. Their selfish ways have turned them to wickedness."

Jonah could not understand why God would tell him about the people of Nineveh for that was a city far away from Galilee, and Jonah did not care what happened there. But the voice continued, this time giving Jonah instructions: "I wish for you to be a messenger for me, Jonah. Tell the people of Nineveh that if they do not change their ways, they will surely bring hard times and punishments on themselves. Go to Nineveh now, Jonah, for great trouble shall come to them in forty days should they continue to live so selfishly. Help them with your words."

"Yes, God, I will do your bidding," said Jonah.

With that, the voice was gone.

Jonah was upset by the unusual request. How could he, an outsider, go to the powerful Assyrian capital and tell people how they ought to be living their lives? Surely, they would think him mad. Jonah felt angry the more he thought about it. "I can make no difference, for they will never listen to me. And why should I help such a cruel and miserable lot? I don't think those people even deserve forgiveness." Jonah felt burdened by God's request and his anger quickly turned to fear: "I cannot go, for the evil people of Nineveh may well kill me."

Before dawn the next day, Jonah quietly left his house and hurried along the road leading to the seaport of Joppa. He was determined not to go to Nineveh. Jonah felt miserable and frightened by his decision; afraid God would see that he was running away.

Upon reaching Joppa, he went to the harbor docks and looked

for a ship readying to depart. Soon he spotted one going to a distant port across the Mediterranean Sea. "What fortune," thought Jonah. "Surely God will never follow me to Tarshish." So he purchased his passage, boarded, and made straightway for the berths below deck. "Down here in the dark of the ship, God will never see me." Jonah believed that as the boat sailed out of land's sight, so too would he be out of God's sight.

Within hours, the sky darkened to a slate-gray, and a great storm came upon them. Forked lightning stabbed the ocean, and massive waves towered about the vessel. Furious winds ripped at the sails and stirred up the sea. The tossing ship began to fill with water and the crew pitched heavy cargo overboard, hoping to lighten the vessel and keep it from sinking. Frantically they chanted prayers, wondering what had angered their gods to such fury.

The shipmaster, not seeing the passenger from Joppa, went searching belowdecks. There he found Jonah sound asleep, obviously unaware there was even a storm. He shook Jonah and said, "Wake up and come above, for a tempest unlike any I have seen has risen up." When the crewmen saw Jonah on deck, they turned to him with suspicion in their eyes. "Who are you that you could sleep through such a storm, and why did you board our ship in the first place?" they questioned, for now the sailors had come to believe that the storm resulted from one person's wickedness. Jonah could not find the words to answer and one sailor yelled at him: "Say your prayers like the rest of us. Ask your god to help us now."

When Jonah seemed incapable of praying, many were angered. "Is it you your god is punishing?" they all wanted to know. Quickly the crewmen drew lots to determine who the guilty aboard was. To no one's surprise, the unlucky draw proved to be Jonah's. Now the sailors turned on Jonah and demanded, "Tell us how have you angered heaven and what will make peace with your god."

Jonah, knowing the truth of the matter, spoke at last: "I have tried to run away from God, but He has found me on the waters. All you can do is save yourselves. Throw me to the stormy sea." The sailors had no wish to cast Jonah into the ocean. They began to row hard toward land, but the sea became wilder all about them. When there seemed no other choice, they hurled Jonah overboard into the raging waves. Immediately the wind stilled and the waters calmed.

Choking on salt water and getting tangled up in long strands of seaweed, Jonah was tossed about violently in the waves. Sure that he would drown, Jonah prepared for the impact of the next enormous wave that he was certain would drive him under to his death. But there before him was a gigantic open mouth flashing its gleaming teeth. Then came a low gasping sound and the waters all about Jonah began to swirl and move forward. He was caught up in a whirling mass that was being powerfully sucked straight toward the beastly mouth – the mouth belonging to a whale. Jonah passed through the horrid cavelike entrance and then, with one gulp, the whale swallowed him whole. Jonah was dragged and tossed about as he spiralled down the giant throat and into the depths of the whale's belly. All was darkness, but Jonah could feel he was surrounded by water, ocean debris, and small swimming fish. The air inside smelled ghastly for half-rotted fish carcasses lay all about. The only sounds were the whale's beating heart and the rush of air as the beast surfaced one last time before descending with its catch to the floor of the ocean.

For three days, Jonah sat in the dank, dark chamber of the whale's belly. He had tried to hide from God and now he was so far away, he felt imprisoned in a tomb. Alone in the darkness, a strange feeling came over Jonah. He felt peaceful and knew God was there. A prayer from the heart came to Jonah's lips:

My dearest God. I cry out to you from the belly of hell and I know you hear my voice. For even when I was cast to the sea and I was dragged to the very depths, still you helped me. For three days and nights my soul has been fading in me, but now it is revived. I know I was wrong. Forgive me, and allow me the chance to go to Nineveh to help the people. I am thankful you are always with me.

Immediately Jonah felt a great shaking, as if he were in the midst of an earthquake. He was thrown around as the whale moved upward toward the surface of the water. A light shone into the belly as the beast opened its jaws. With one gigantic heave, Jonah was pushed up through the dark tunnel of the whale's throat toward the daylight. He was spewed out of the whale's mouth and landed in shallow seawaters. Jonah waded to shore, then fell to his knees. "Thank you, God," he wept.

Jonah was to keep his promise to God. Three days he journeyed with a joyful heart. He spoke to the people of Nineveh and his words were received, for they were spoken with newly gained wisdom and compassion. Thus, the people of Nineveh changed and were spared their own ordeal.

THE MIDGARD SERPENT

An ice age, an ax age, a sword age, and a wind age.
Then a wolf age bringing battle.
Odin shall fight the mighty wolf, Fenrir.
The All-Father shall be devoured in battle.
Thor, mighty though he be, shall fight a battle to the death
With the fearsome sea serpent, Jormungand.
Gods, monsters, and giants shall meet their deaths together.

THIS WAS THE ANCIENT PROPHECY FORETOLD by Mimir, the Norse god of wisdom and prophecy, at the beginning of time. His message of doom and destruction was set into grim motion from the outset of the Norse universe. All was drama and chaos with the collision of two opposing forces: one of ice and one of fire. And the impact formed a huge giant from whom sprang all life – his body became the earth and his flowing blood, the seas.

The Norse world was divided into nine realms. Midgard was the world of men. Asgard, home of the gods, was overseen by Odin, the All-Father.

Destructive forces came to Asgard early. Loki, god of fire and ruler of the underworld, was father to three monstrous children – beasts who were to bring ruin to all the gods. Fenrir, the oldest, was a hideous wolf creature; Hel was a hag of death; and Jormungand, a vicious serpent. The All-Father, knowing the evil nature of these gruesome siblings, secretly arranged for Loki's children to be captured and brought to his court. There, Odin decided they should all be sent far away, where they would be of less direct danger to the gods. Hel the hag was shipped to the realm of Niflheim, where she was surrounded by misery, dead bodies, and evil mists. Fenrir the wolf was tied up, gagged, and sent to live on a remote island. But Jormungand the serpent was hurled around and around in the air and sent flying into the world of men. The monster landed in the depths of the icy northern seas.

So massive was he in the world of men that, although he lurked beneath the waters, his body when stretched out encircled the entire earth, with his tail coming to rest in his mouth. Just by moving, the sea serpent could stir up violent commotion in the world's waters. Because his monstrous form coiled in a stranglehold around the earth, he was called the World Serpent, or the Midgard Serpent.

Only one god in Asgard could match the strength of this

hideous serpent. Odin's son Thor was indeed the mightiest of all the gods. His power was seen in the earthly skies as he hurled lightning bolts, for he was the god of thunder. Thor was a burly red-headed and bearded god who, while not of the highest intellect, was full of tremendous energy and absolute fearlessness. Should his great strength ever weaken, Thor wore a belt of might and special gloves that gave his hands the power to crumble boulders. But his most prized possession was the stone hammer, which Thor called Mjollnir. It was as mighty as a meteorite and had the power of a lightning bolt. With it, Thor crushed many a giant's evil skull.

For all his simplemindedness and stubborn willpower, Thor could never pass up a good challenge. As far as Thor was concerned, there was no worthier calling than to bring an end to the Midgard Serpent. As long as Thor breathed life, for the Norse gods – though powerful – were not immortals, his greatest mission was to kill Jormungand.

Thor's plan was to go in disguise to the hall of the great sea giant Hymir. Hymir did not cotton on to who he was entertaining, even when Thor ate two whole oxen at the dinner table that night. The next morning when Hymir left early to go fishing, Thor followed him, for he wanted to find the Midgard Serpent. Catching up to Hymir, Thor called out: "I beg you, good Hymir, allow me to go out on the waters with you this fine day." The sea giant could see no harm in the matter and agreed. Thor readied the boat, secretly planning how he would lure his monstrous catch. "Good Hymir," Thor shouted from the shore, "I have lined up the hooks and fishing lines, but can find only small worms for bait. I want to catch something worthy of your stature to repay your kindness. Where might I find bigger bait?" Hymir shrugged his enormous shoulders, so Thor took matters into his own hands. He bounded across the fields and grabbed one of Hymir's bulls in a death grip. Then, with one tug, he hauled off the beast's head.

Hymir was enraged, screaming: "By the gods, man, do you know what crime you have committed? You have ripped the head off my prize ox, Heavenly Bellower." Thor pretended to take no notice and got quickly into the boat, leaving Hymir no choice but to follow. The thunder god, with his almighty strength, gave one haul on the oars and the boat sped rapidly from shore. Within seconds Hymir announced they were at his fishing spot, but Thor continued rowing. Hymir pleaded: "Only stop now for we are heading straight for danger. Do you not know that beneath these waters lurks the Midgard Serpent?" Thor threw back his head and, laughing in defiance, brought the boat to a stop, pulled up his oars, and baited his fishing line with the head of Heavenly Bellower.

Thor tossed the line over the side of the boat, laughing boisterously. "This should be a short wait with such a great delicacy dangling about," he said aloud. Hymir gasped and sank to the floor of the boat, for he had great fear of the sea serpent. Sure enough, within a minute, a gigantic tug rocked the vessel, for Jormungand had let go of his own tail to lift his ugly head up toward the dangling ox head. With one gulp he was caught on the end of Thor's line. The hook had pierced the roof of the serpent's enormous mouth. There was great pulling, thrashing about, and wrenching from the end of the line, but Thor held on tight. It was a great battle of strength that brought the thunder god to his knees. Still he held fast to the line.

Then, with a crash, part of the boat bottom gave way and Thor found himself with his feet flatly on the floor of the ocean. With one gigantic yank, he pulled the serpent up out of the water. He was face to face, locked in a death glare, with the most gruesome of creatures. Neither Thor nor the Midgard Serpent blinked an eye.

By now Hymir was in a state of utter panic. At the moment Thor reached his hand down to grasp his hammer to kill the serpent, Hymir gave in to his terror and cut loose the line, releasing Jormungand back into the sea. When Thor looked up, Jormungand had vanished below the churned-up waters. Enraged, Thor made a fist and, with all of his brute strength, gave Hymir such a blow it sent the sea giant overboard into the waters. Without so much as a look back to see how the sea giant was faring, Thor walked along the sea bottom back to shore.

A long time was to pass before Thor and Jormungand were to fight again. It would be the final battle, as the ancient prophecy had foretold. The two adversaries would meet at Ragnarok, where a giant battle of good and evil between the gods of Asgard and the monstrous children would occur. For many years, Fenrir had waited on his island for the death combat, while Hel had waited in her deathly court, and Jormungand lurked in the depths of the earth's sea.

Without great warning, the prophecy began to come true as Mimir, the god of wisdom and prophecy, had foretold:

A winter came that showed no signs of letting up. In fact, it was the Ice Age – three years of endless winter. The evil children of Loki and their monstrous allies were gathering forces: Fenrir the wolf snatched the very sun out of the heavens and swallowed it whole. The Midgard Serpent was writhing with monstrous glee beneath the waters. The shores were pounded with high waves as Jormungand thrashed about, eager to meet his enemies. On those furious seas a crew of giants sailed to the battlegrounds aboard the ghastly ship *Naglfar*, a boat made of dead men's fingernails and launched by Hel.

Mimir had warned the gods that when Heimdall, their watch-man, sounded his horn, it was the call to the last battle. Fenrir and Jormungand made their way together. The wolf belched flames and Jormungand spat poisonous venom. The world was coming to a gruesome end, as the prophecy had foretold.

Odin drew his sword and fought with the mighty wolf Fenrir and Mimir's ancient words were played out:

The All-Father shall be devoured in battle.
Thor, mighty though he be, shall fight a battle to the death
With the fearsome sea serpent, Jormungand.

Thor fought on in the bloody battle with the Midgard Serpent. He called on all his godly strength and the power of his magic belt and gloves, and still the ugly sea serpent writhed in his grip. Finally Thor held Jormungand secure and, with one crack to the skull, slayed the serpent. But prophecy had foretold Thor's death. Not realizing he was acting out the prophecy's ending, Thor stepped nine paces back and at that moment the serpent, with one horrendous last gasp of death, spewed up venomous poison. The fumes filled the air and Thor inhaled the fatal vapors.

Mimir's words echoed over the battlefield that day:

Gods, monsters, and giants shall meet their deaths together.
The fire giant, Surt, shall scorch the earth with his
flaming sword.
All shall be ablaze; then shall come flood.
The flaming ball of the earth shall sink into the sea.
The stars shall fall from the sky and there will be only
darkness.
But behold, a day shall come when a new earth will rise
from the water –
A pure, green earth lit by a new and radiant sun.
For in the ending has come the beginning.

THE KRAKEN

Below the thunders of the upper deep;
Far, far beneath in the abysmal sea,
His ancient, dreamless, uninvaded sleep
The Kraken sleepeth.

— Alfred, Lord Tennyson

THREE CENTURIES AGO OFF THE COAST OF Norway, a giant sea monster reared its ugly head, and word spread that the Kraken was indeed the largest creature in all the world's oceans. Norwegian fishermen came to fear their own waters and sailors were ever alert when sailing several miles off the coast. They were especially vigilant on hot summer days as the heat was more likely to draw the beast to the surface.

The first indication of the Kraken's presence was a sudden

change in the water's depth; the ocean would become shallower than the sailors knew it ought to be. Sometimes a shoal rose out of the water, where none was charted on a map. Then, longtime fishermen took to rowing hard. To them it meant the vicious Kraken was waking up beneath the waters and soon the spikes of its mile-long back would rise with the sea grasses from the ocean floor.

As the massive creature stirred, the water began to swirl and circle into eddies that spanned for miles around. "'Tis the Kraken in its Maelstrom" was how the sailors read the startling appearance of whirlpools and whitecaps all about them. Row as they might, their ship had only to get caught and spun about to come

into the clutches of the surfacing sea monster. The sailors prepared for the true terror to unleash itself on them.

The splash of a giant wave signalled the rise of the Kraken, head and all. Its hideous tentacled arms swept up into the air, some of them reaching high into the masts of the largest vessels. The Kraken clung on with a death grip, pulling on the boat and sucking it into its fierce whirlpool, the Maelstrom, down to its lair at the bottom of the sea.

There hath he lain for ages and will lie . . .
In roaring he shall rise and on the surface die.
        – Alfred, Lord Tennyson

DRAGON KINGS OF THE SEA

Deep in the oceans of Ancient China lived four Dragon Kings of the Sea and their dragon wives. Each ruled one of the four seas, for it was believed then that the earth was surrounded on each of its four directions by a sea. Some believed that there were in fact five Dragon Kings, the fifth being a king of kings who resided in the center of the others.

THE DRAGON KINGS WERE BROTHERS. AO SHUN ruled the Northern Sea, while Ao Ch'in governed the Southern Sea; Ao Kuang was in the East and Ao Jun, the West. Each Dragon King was a different color – the dragon in the North was black; the dragon in the South was red; the East dragon was blue; and West dragon was white. The Dragon Kings of the Sea had sharp claws and scales of armor. They could belch smoke and flame that had, at times, charred passing fish that came too close. Each was of such monstrous proportions that its movements shook the earth; hurricanes flared up and waterspouts formed in the seas overhead.

The Dragon Kings of the Sea lived in crystal palaces at the bottom of their oceans. Each Dragon King had a large court and was personally attended to by ministers of the court. An army, made up of fish and crabs, was on constant duty patrolling the underwater world.

The Dragon Kings of the Sea were revered for their secret knowledge. Being healers, they sometimes surfaced with cures for a village in need and were thought to bring good fortune.

But often they brought terror. If, after a meal of pearls and opals, a contented Dragon King dozed off underwater, tidal waves could build up until typhoons raged. If angered, the Dragon Kings of the Sea sent storms to whip up the waters and blow across the shores. Only offerings to the powerful Dragon Kings could restore calm.

SCYLLA AND CHARYBDIS

He runs on Scylla to avoid Charybdis.
— Virgil

The azure blue Mediterranean appears tranquil, but that inviting-looking sea posed a terrifying threat to ancient sailors. The Strait of Messina leading into Sicily was a perilous passage, for there dwelt two of the most fiendish sea monsters the world had known. Once a mariner's course was set for the strait, there was no escaping those sea beasts. No matter how well a sailor navigated, the passage was a guaranteed watery grave for many of the crew. A sailor could merely choose his fate between Scylla, the six-headed man-eating monster, on one side and Charybdis, the devouring whirlpool, on the other. This hideous pair had not always been sea beasts. Their story is as sad and tragic as the fate of the mariners whose lives they claimed.

SCYLLA HAD STARTED LIFE AS A COMELY MAIDEN. She loved the warm Sicilian waters and every day she would go to a small bay off the shore to bathe.

Scylla was unaware of being watched from a distance. Glaucus had not meant to spy on her that day, but when he saw Scylla in the bay he was captivated. "Such grace and beauty I have not seen in another," he gasped, and his heart melted. In a fit of passion he leaped from the bushes. "Young maiden, I know not who you are, but I do know that from the moment I saw you, I loved you deeply," he declared.

Scylla looked up from the water and shrieked from both surprise and repulsion. Standing before her was not a man but a triton, with long seaweed-green hair, skin the color of the ocean, and a scaly fish tail. "How can such an offensive creature be declaring his love?" Scylla wondered.

Glaucus, seeing her alarm, explained how he came to look as he did. "My dear lady, do not fear me. Not so very long ago I was a hardworking fisherman. Then one day I stopped at an island to shake the day's catch out of my net, and my life changed." Still sensing the girl's distress, he hurried along to further his explanation. "Having set the fish on the grass, I was amazed to see that, though minutes before they had been gasping for breath, they suddenly began to wriggle. Before my eyes, they completely revived and, with tremendous jumps, each and every fish flung itself back into the sea. So curious was this to me that I inspected the grass the fish had lain upon. I brought a blade to my lips, then tasted it.

Instantly I began to quiver and my body transformed into what you now see before you."

Scylla looked sadly moved by his story and Glaucus thought she might cry. Immediately he reassured her: "Do not feel sorry for me, for with this change I was filled with a deep and wonderful yearning to live in the sea. I followed that call and the great Poseidon has embraced me as a triton."

Scylla, although strangely moved by his story, looked straight into the triton's eyes and ran from the water. "You cannot love me as you say for I can never, never return your affection," she yelled back to Glaucus. "Pray leave me alone that I may come again to enjoy the waters of this bay in privacy."

The triton, however, was smitten and sought the help of Circe, the great enchantress, to win the heart of Scylla. Unbeknownst to Glaucus, Circe had no intention of helping him, for she herself was decidedly drawn to the young triton and was enraged at Scylla's neglect of so sweet and loveable a creature.

Circe vowed her revenge on Scylla, and dark and horrible was its form. That night she concocted a magical brew of bitter herbs. "May she, who is so repulsed by the triton, find out what it is to be truly monstrous," she cursed as she hurried with her elixir to the Bay of Sicily. By moonlight, Circe poured her evil mixture into the waters and waited for the maiden to come for her bath.

Just after dawn, Scylla arrived and waded into the poisonous seawater. Immediately she sprouted twelve gangly feet and long grotesque tails. She glided her fingers through the water and her hands became scaly claws. Then she dipped her whole body into the warm salty sea. Up sprang six long snaky necks, each with a frightful beast head, with three rows of sharp and grisly animal teeth.

Gone too was the maiden's innocent spirit. Scylla now had a monster's nature and strong killing instincts. She plunged deep into the sea and swam with a beast's strength until she came to the opening of the bay. She hollowed out a cavern in a rockface and sank into it up to her waist. There she remained planted, ever waiting for unsuspecting sailors passing through the busy sea-lane. As soon as they came within her grasp, she reached forward to sweep them from the deck with her powerful claws. Her six heads would then descend swiftly and each savage mouth would pluck up a man from the bench of rowers. The sailors struggled to release themselves from her gruesome jaws, but no one ever escaped. Their lives ended in one hideous crunch of her powerful teeth or, even more horrible, those unfortunate enough to be dragged away to her lair to be stored until her hunger struck again had their deaths prolonged.

Believe it or not, Scylla was the less bleak of the two prospects, for to choose Charybdis was to decide upon certain death for the entire crew and guaranteed wreckage of the vessel. This ever thirsty whirlpool had also once been a maiden, but hers is not as innocent a story as Scylla's.

Unlike the graceful Scylla, whose only crime was being envied by a sorceress, Charybdis was cursed by her own folly and greed. She was a spoiled and pampered princess who demanded her every wish be obliged and done so immediately. While this was difficult enough for the people who attended her, it was unbearable to the immortals. Such behavior was not tolerated by them.

One day, her actions offended the goddess Demeter. Charybdis, in her willfulness, ignored the pleas of a forest dryad to let the trees alone. For disregarding nature, Charybdis was taught a hard lesson.

Demeter sent the curse of famine down to earth in the disguise of a large fig growing on the tree outside of Charybdis' window. Next morning, when the princess awoke, the mouthwatering fruit seemed to beckon her. The servant girl noticed the fig and remarked how plump and succulent it looked. Since she was so hungry, she asked if she might have it. But the selfish princess leaped from her bed, grabbed it from the servant's hands, and popped it into her mouth. No sooner had Charybdis swallowed it than a never-ending hunger and an unquenchable thirst took hold.

The princess stuffed her face with every morsel of food she could find. Still hungry, she moved to her father's pastures, where she began to devour whole sheep and cows. Her appetite grew greater and more terrible. She began attacking people in their homes.

At this point the mightiest of gods looked down on her destruction and decided to remove the bloodthirsty menace far from temptation. He sent down a blast of wind that began spinning the obese spiteful princess round and round at a furious rate. It lifted her off the ground and whirled her through the air until she came to the Strait of Messina, across from the monstrous Scylla. There, it plunked her into the waters and she was confined to her place by a large rock marked by a fig tree.

Still her terrible thirst demanded to be quenched. Three times a day she drank the tides, swallowing all that passed overhead. Each time, she completely drained the waters so that the mud of sea bottom was visible. Then, with one horrendous blast, Charybdis spit the waters back out and the force of the torrent formed a whirlpool in a huge area around her rock. Any ship passing nearby was sucked into the vortex and swallowed up. So great was the impact that it pulverized whole vessels into splinters in an instant and the violent force caught the crewmen, sucking them down to their deaths.

The twin curse of Scylla and Charybdis was the dilemma of every mariner sailing the strait between Italy and Sicily. Navigating that narrow passageway always was made at the great cost of human lives. To spare as many sailors as possible required skill and daring. The only workable solution for most sailors was to run "on Scylla to avoid Charybdis."

III

ENCHANTING MELODIES: MERFOLK

MERMAID SIGHTING

This morning, one of our companie looking over boord saw a Mermaid, and calling up some of the companie to see her, one more came up, and by that time shee was come close to the ship's side, looking earnestly on the men: a little after, a Sea came and overturned her: From the Navill upward, her backe and breasts were like a womans (as they say that saw her) her body as big as one of us; her skin very white; and long haire hanging down behinde, of colour blacke; in her going downe they saw her tayle, which was like the tayle of a Porposse, and speckled like a Macrell. Their names that saw her were Thomas Hilles and Robert Raynar.

– From the logbook of Henry Hudson, June 15, 1608.

THE BLUE MEN
OF THE MINCH

Oh, weary of the Blue Men, their anger and their wiles.
The whole day long, the whole night long,
*   they splash around the isles;*
They follow every fisher – ah! they haunt the fisher's
*   dream –*
When billows toss, oh, who would cross the Blue Men's
*   Stream?*

                           – Minch boatman's song

THE ISLANDS OF THE HEBRIDES PEPPER THE rugged and tempestuous seas off the Highlands of Scotland. A narrow strait runs between two of the most northerly islands – Lewis and the Shant Isles. Now the Shant Isles are often called the Charmed Islands. The strait has a nickname, but one that reflects treachery – not charm. Sometimes local fishermen call it the Current of Destruction, but more likely you would hear them talk of avoiding the Blue Men's Stream.

In these Outer Hebridean waters live curious and malevolent mermen who are known to churn up fearsome waves. They create chaotic storms to swamp those ships foolhardy enough to venture through the strait. These mermen are as wild and rugged in appearance as the seas they inhabit. Their large strong bodies have a deep bluish gray tinge; their faces are expressive and stormy, framed with foamy beards, sea-blue hair, and eyebrows encrusted in salt spray. They are the Blue Men of the Minch.

The clan of the Blue Men and their chieftain live in caves along the ocean floor. When they are in their dwellings deep below the waves, the channel is serene. As the Blue Men surface for a day of wild sport, the waters begin to churn. They love to skim through the ocean at rapid speeds, bobbing to the surface and splashing up a storm as they slap the seas with their long blue arms. The strait is their playground and they teach any ship that intrudes a long drawn-out lesson.

Most boats avoid the Minch, choosing to forgo the shorter passage and sail all the way around the Shant Isles. For even when the channel looks peaceful, the waters can be restless in no time. Calm seas mean only that the Blue Men are resting in their caves. Usually one of their sentinels is on duty just beneath the water's surface. When a vessel approaches, he dives down to inform his clan of the intruders.

The strength of the Blue Men is legendary. They can bring a ship to a dead stop with one hand stretched up through the waters. The skipper aboard knows it's time to pay attention to every detail of the ensuing exchange. While the Blue Men could flip the ship in an instant, they don't. Not right away, that is. For just as much as they love splashing through the spray do they enjoy a good verbal match in the form of a rhyming contest.

If the boat's skipper is dull-witted and has no ear for verse, the ship is most certainly doomed. The Blue Men start up the contest of words with two lines. It is then up to the skipper to respond with a couplet that rhymes. A lot is at stake for the crew, for all is lost when the skipper cannot supply the last word. The Blue Men lift the ship from the water, shake it high in the air, and hurl it like a javelin until it lands and sinks into the Minch.

Few have successfully met the Blue Men's challenge, but those who did recorded their contest so others might know of the strange skills required to cross the strait. A poetry match with these articulate mermen has been known to go like this:

MacLeod, Mackay, from the Isle of Skye
Dare you to cross my strait?

Aye, there, Blue Man, I do indeed
Or else my ship runs late.

Your ship it shall not pass at all
Unless you rhyme my verse.

Well let's get on for time's agoin'.
I'm ready to converse.

You think you're clever, skipper man,
And you'll never me outwit.

I'll drum my fingers while I think
And drive you to a fit.

Be still and speak in smarter rhymes.
You see I shake your hull.

You rock my boat by sheer brute strength.
No way you'll rock my skull.

Methinks you fancy you have won.
I'll plunge you 'neath the waves.

Should you but break your fair play rules
My ghost will avenge your caves.

The Blue Men of the Minch know when a battle of words is fairly lost. On the chieftain's signal the clan dives down below the waves, the surface waters calm, and the victorious captain and his ship are allowed safe passage through the Minch.

THE SEA PEOPLE

I am a man upon the land
I am a selkie in the sea
And when I'm far from every strand
My dwelling is in Sule Skerrie.

– From "The Grey Selkie of Sule Skerrie"

THIS VERSE IS FROM A HAUNTING BALLAD SUNG in the Outer Hebrides of Scotland. Sule Skerrie is a rock that sits out in the seas off the southwest coast of the Orkney Islands. Seals love to gather on that lone skerrie and bask in the warmth of the sun. Their sounds carry over the waves to the folk on the island shore. The stories passed down about the seals that came to shore as people have become as much a part of island life as the constant crashing of waves all about.

Some folk think the sea people are the souls of those who have drowned at sea. Others believe the selkies are fallen angels. Stories about them are marked by regret and sad choices the seal woman had to make, while selkie songs and ballads are most often laments.

THE SELKIE WOMAN

One evening in late June, a young man was out walking after a long day of mackerel fishing. The seashore was lit by the splendid full moon on the rise. In the moonlight, the familiar rocks, sand, and waters of the cove appeared strange to his eyes. He felt he was walking along a very different beach than that of his own North Uist isle shore. Perhaps the shore was transformed, for this June night was none other than Midsummer's Eve. The young man had given no thought to the stories the older folk had told about the magics of Midsummer – a time they said spirits and enchantments could present themselves to common folk. The Outer Hebrides were full of such tales, yet the young man thought that one night was surely the same as another. He was out for a late-night stroll and nothing more. He was certainly not expecting anything out of the ordinary to appear, so at first the laughter and singing he heard coming from down the shore did not strike him as peculiar in the least. . . .

UNWITTINGLY HE FOLLOWED THE MUSIC, and soon realized he had walked a long distance down the beach at this late hour. But the merriment seemed to be coming from the rocks ahead, and now he was curious to see the source. He made his way quickly down the shore and peaked around the boulders.

In the shelter of a small cove, on the glistening wet sand, he saw a group of lovely women dancing in a circle. They laughed and sang as they spun about in the moonlight. The young man quickly figured out who they were.

The old folk spoke of the sea people – the selkies, they called them – who danced on the shores every Midsummer's Eve. The young man had not believed that a seal could shed its skin, let alone come ashore in human form. But he could clearly see sealskins lying on top of the rocks and on the sand across from where he watched the women dance. He remembered other selkie stories and quietly crept along the beach in the shadows of the large rocks. When he came to the first sealskin, he bent down and picked it up and hid it inside his coat. The sudden movement startled one of the sea people and, in an instant, the Midsummer spell was broken. The dancing and singing stopped. There was great confusion and wild cries as the seal maidens all ran to find their sealskins.

With loud splashing, they all dived from the rocks back into the sea. All of the seal maidens, that is, but one. She dashed from rock to rock and across the stretch of sand, looking for her sealskin. She ran desperately to the shore and, stretching her long white arms out to sea, called to her seal friends to wait for her. They answered in distressed cries, then slipped out of sight under the waves. The seal maiden crumpled to the wet sand and began to weep in sounds of deep despair.

The young man moved out of the shadows and hurried to the shore. He stood calmly above the seal maiden sitting in the sea foam covered with her long dark hair. He knew he had never gazed at such beauty, for indeed her beauty was not of this earth. She looked up at him with pleading eyes – deep brown pools welling up with tears. She was meltingly beautiful and he knew right there and then that he loved her.

The pretty seal maiden cried out: "Kind sir, I can see you have my sealskin. Take pity and give it back to me, for without it I can never return to the sea, the home that I love." Then once again she wept a pitiful lament, wringing her hands in great distress.

The young man loved her, but remained untouched by her pleas. He had already decided this was the woman he would marry, and surely she would thank him one day for the comforts of land living. "Dear and gentle lady," the young man began, "I want you for my wife. I promise you a happy life ashore, where you will always be warm and cared for. Stand up, sweet lady, and come with me."

She looked at him and saw that he was resolved to have it so. There was nothing she could do, for he held her only way back to the sea. "Promise me one thing then, sir," begged the seal maiden.

"Take good care of my sealskin for should harm come to it, so it should also come to me."

"Now that I can promise you, for I have no desire to lose you," said the young man. He clutched the sealskin tightly in his one hand, and put it behind his back. The seal maiden slowly rose and the man took off his coat. She shuddered as he put his coat over her shoulders. Together they walked back to the small village.

The young man remembered the words of the old people's stories: "One must only marry a selkie maiden on the third night after finding her." So it was they were married and the young man brought his new bride to his little thatched cottage, a humble dwelling streaked with mud and sea salt from the constant batter of wind and sea spray. Inside it was cosy enough and the seal woman found herself with all the comforts she had been promised. The fire in the large stone hearth was kept going all day to keep out the dampness. She thought it a lovely sight, for it reminded her of the sun's red glow as it set above her on the horizon, when she had been in her dear sea. When she yearned for her sea home, she looked straight into the glow and found some small measure of comfort.

It was not that she was miserable. As time went on, the husband felt quite certain she was actually enjoying being his wife and mother of their seven children. Indeed, she was as good and hardworking a wife as any woman in the village. She kept a neat cottage, baked bread, and seemed to draw pleasure from spinning wool from the fleece of the small flock of sheep she tended.

The village folk who came to visit thought her to be a most gentle woman, if somewhat on the quiet and shy side. All remarked on her loveliness. Her black shiny hair hung beautifully about her rounded face. But it was those eyes – enormous and mild, a deep velvety brown one second, then dancing wildly with every hue the next. At times they were the eyes of deep intelligence, but there was a hint of pain and sorrow when the seal woman gazed up, unaware of being caught in thought. Some noticed the slight webbing between her fingers, the roughness of her palms, and the slowness of her breathing. These were sure signs of a selkie woman and the talk spread. One of the old women of Uist thought she had a look of deep knowing, and it was common knowledge that selkie women could read into the future and foretell events. Another old woman told the village folk that the seal woman had the eyes of a bewitched soul desiring release from its prison.

The seal woman kept mostly to herself and stayed busy with running her home and bringing up the "wee bairns," as she had been taught to refer to her children. All seven of her little ones showed a great liking for the sea, and were excellent swimmers and divers. The seal woman loved her children and when they were ill, she used her sea people's knowledge of medicine to heal them. Often she stared out the cottage window that faced the shore, and her husband feared what might be holding her in such deep thought. He had grown to love her greatly and remembered with reluctance the warnings in the selkie stories: "The selkie women may make good wives and mothers, but they never lose their love of the sea."

Throughout the years they did not speak about the sealskin, but the husband kept the promise he had made to his wife. He cared for it – preserving it well and keeping it in dry places where dampness would not spoil it. He checked from time to time that it kept its sheen and softness. The sealskin was not an easy thing for him to keep hidden, but every year he found a new hiding place. One time he hid it high in the eaves of the cottage; another time he locked it in his sea chest and made sure to always carry the key with him. Now he thought it safely hidden under a high stack of hay.

One afternoon, when the husband was out fishing in the waters off the island, the wife sent her children out to play before supper. It was hot in the cottage from bread baking and they were happy to run outside in the cool autumn air. A game of hide-and-seek was soon underway. The seal woman watched out the window as six of her little ones scattered while the oldest one counted, then searched. She continued with her cooking, but great shouts from outside soon interrupted her. Fearing someone was hurt, she dashed out the cottage door.

"Mother, come quickly. Wee James has found a dead animal buried up in the haystack." She ran to the field and looked down at her smallest child crying in the hay. "Mother, only look," he sobbed, "just the fur and nothing more."

The seal woman gasped when she knelt to examine it. It was not the fur of a cat or dog, but her very own sealskin. She looked at it, then said, "It is all right, my wee darlings. Be off to play and I will look after this matter." She watched as they headed off, then looked down again at her precious sealskin. How long she had waited for this moment; now she trembled to touch it. All about her felt like a pleasant dream. Her sweet children's voices seemed far away, the little cottage faint in the distance. She stroked the sealskin lovingly and the waves suddenly crashed loudly on the shore below the field. She dared not pick it up; she must turn back to the cottage. "Ah, wee lads and lassies of my heart, I canna leave ye." And she sobbed, for the sound of the waves grew louder all about her.

She held up the sealskin and the smell of the sea was still there. At that moment a wind brought the wild smell of the sea up from the beach, and with it, the sound of the surf pounding on the sand. She ran swiftly to the shore. She held the skin in her arms, then cried aloud back toward the cottage. The children stopped their playing and listened to their gentle mother's voice in the wind. "My sweet bairns," she said, "I must be leaving you to return to my home in the sea, for there I have seven other children. Remember, my wee land dearies, that I will love you and look out for you always. Each day when you walk along the shore, look out on the sea. I will rise out of the waters to see you. I promise to leave fish and small treasures from the ocean on the rocks for you every day. And I will keep you and your father safe on the waters. Say good-bye to him for me and tell him he was a good man to me all these years. I love you all."

At that moment the father was returning in his boat from a day's fishing. The children ran weeping to the shore. They shouted, but their mother could no longer hear their voices – she heard only waves. They watched and none could stop her, for it was as if the tide itself was pulling her in. She put on her sealskin and dived into the sea. Far offshore a great seal appeared and called out to her. Her song back to him was one of sheer joy. He waited for her to come to him, then together they disappeared under the waves.

As their mother had told them to do, the children went down to the sea in the mornings. Always on the rocks they found fish for their day's meal, and little shells and pretty stones. Then they heard their mother's sweet and joyful sea song. When they looked out over the waters they would always see the same beautiful seal appear, bob about for a while, then dive beneath the waves. Often when they walked along the beach, they found mysterious treasures washed ashore. They knew their dear mother was looking out for them.

The father too felt her presence when he was out fishing. He definitely had more luck than ever before in his days' catches, and his boat navigated safely through the fiercest of storms. Once a seal swam near his boat and, when he looked carefully, he was sure he saw large tears in its mild brown eyes.

The seal woman never returned to her family in human form, but her children grew up to become great healers and could tell people's fortunes. There was a strange beauty to them and many a village story concerned them. Some said they had webbing between their fingers and toes, and scaly patches of skin – the markings of a selkie woman's descendants. In North Uist, the isle folk called them *Silochd nan Ron*, which simply meant "the offspring of the seals."

MERMAID LORE

Who would be a mermaid fair,
Singing alone, combing her hair
Under the sea in a golden curl
With a comb of pearl on a throne?
 – From "The Mermaid" by Alfred, Lord Tennyson

Mermaid Lore:
Mermaids were believed to be in the form of a woman from the
waist up, with the rest of their bodies being long and slender
silvery green fish tails. They were renowned for their great beauty,
with deep watery blue eyes and long golden hair that hung all
about them. Word was that mermaids kept their maidenly beauty
for they were eternally young. They were spotted on tidal ledges,
rocks, or swimming about in the waters.

   Mermaids loved to sing and were often enthralled by human

music. Frequently they sat on rocks overlooking their sea homes. There they would sit singing with their magical voices, while basking in the sun or enjoying the moonlight. They gazed at themselves in a glass (mirror) as they combed their long hair. Their mirrors were said to be of glistening gold with handles of pearls. Some mermaids came to the craggy shore to spread out white linens to dry in the sun. Others played their music on harps and lyres. Always they sang with voices of unearthly beauty.

The sea homes of mermaids were reckoned to be as beautiful, mysterious, and enchanting as the creatures themselves. On the ocean floor were underwater castles of coral and pearl and crystal caves. Jewelled gardens and kelp forests were all about and the mermaids' homes were very much underwater fairylands. Mermaids were thought to keep magical herds of sea cattle and sheep beneath the waves.

To travel between the elements and survive in both water and air, mermaids required magic objects. Sometimes a shawl or veil draped over their head and shoulders allowed the special trip from sea to earth. Irish mermaids called Merrows wore enchanted caps called the *cohulleen druith*. The caps were red in color and often sported long red feathers. Some Hebridean mermaids wore silver belts to give them the power to return to the depths; others had vials of ointment in their possession, which they smeared on their skin. If a mermaid became stranded on a shore because of a sudden tidal change, she was often forced to live with the human who stole her magic object. Like the selkie women, mermaids could live useful and dutiful shore lives, but always yearned to return to the sea. This was only possible upon finding the magic object that gave them the power to go back.

Mermaid stories, while similar in many ways, vary slightly on every shore where they are told. Like the magic objects associated with different mermaids, so too are they known by other names: Mere-Mayde, Merrow, Morgan, Mama Alo, and Ningyo are but a few.

Mermaid Tears:
Some thought mermaids came near to humans at sea and onshore to search for a soul, the belief being that mermaids were fallen angels without souls. A tale is told on the Scottish isle of Iona of

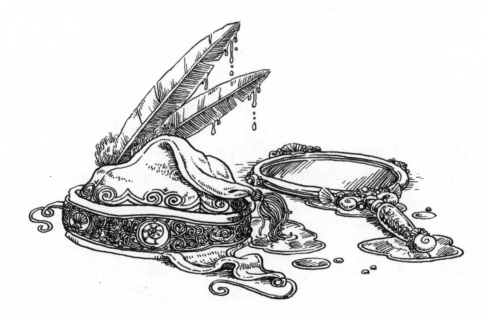

a dear little mermaid who came to the island shore daily to ask for a soul. She was always denied. She begged, pleaded, and cried but to no avail. Eventually the little mermaid returned to the sea for good, but behind on the island one can still see her tears. The grayish green shore pebbles found only on Iona's shore are called mermaid's tears.

> *How sad a welcome!*
> *Some ragged child holds up for sale, a store*
> *Of wave-worn pebbles, pleading on the shore.*
> — William Wordsworth's poetic
> reflections of arriving on Iona

Mermaid Superstitions:

Here are some beliefs passed down over the years regarding mermaids:

- Mermaids appear on the water just before a storm.
- Mermaids play with fish before a storm. If they throw a fish through the air in a direction away from the ship, it means that the ship's crew will survive the storm. If, however, they throw a fish toward the ship, there will be one or more deaths.
- Mermaids often dance on the waves in anticipation of the excitement a fierce storm brings.
- Mermaids weep when the weather stays fine, and sing when a tempest approaches.

- People who help a stranded mermaid, or aid in her freedom, can be richly rewarded. A mermaid might repay a kindness with the granting of three wishes, the forewarning of storms at sea, or the imparting of her knowledge of herbal remedies. Sometimes she bestows special gifts – most often the gifts of music, healing, and fortune-telling. Other times she might repay a helpful human with gems and riches from shipwrecks. Some have singled out a person or, in certain cases, whole villages for their favors, bestowing on them riches and good fortune.

- Should a mermaid feel wronged or rejected, her vengeance is quick and merciless. She curses those people who have harmed her. In anger she has been known to blow whole roofs off houses, completely block up the mouth of a harbor with sand, drown people, and unleash killer waves that only strike the person she has targeted. Some say she has driven certain people utterly mad.

- Mermaids can raise tempests by singing, or by knotting their long hair.

- Mermaids can both predict and control storms.

- Mermaids can foretell the future.

- When sailors throw objects – usually knives – at a mermaid, if she remains floating, they consider themselves safe.

- In the Philippines, good fortune on the water can be secured if three golden hairs are plucked from a sleeping mermaid's head.

- Sailors believe that a mermaid's song can enchant them and should they hear it, they will be drawn by some irresistible force to their deaths in the seas. Navigators worry the entire crew could be pulled to follow and the ship would then be wrecked on the rocks.

When up it raise the mermaiden
With a comb and glass in her hand:
"Here's a health to you, my merry young men,
For you never will see dry land!"

                    – Anon.

IV

BOLD BALLADS:
TALL TALES AND
FANTASTIC
VOYAGES

MISTER STORMALONG

An able sailor, bold and true
To my way, you storm along,
A good old bosun to his crew.
Ay, ay, ay, Mister Stormalong.
  – Sea chantey

WHEN THE FOGHORN IS BLARING OFF-
shore, 'tis a time when old sea captains love
to tell yarns. But along Cape Cod, captains
are more apt to be telling tall tales. For how
else can one tell a story about a larger-than-life seaman like
Mister Stormalong? The way they tell it, Stormalong was a maritime Paul Bunyon.

The legend of Mister Stormalong begins that day he first appeared on the cape. "'Twas the hurricane of 1826" is how folk always tell it in those parts, "and a huge tidal wave came crashing in on our blessed cape's shore."

For the longest time after the sea had calmed, folk along the coast continued to hear blustery howling and deep wails. Knowing that "the gale had blowed itself out," they ran to the shore to see what manner of sea beast had washed up. So powerful was the creature's cry, they thought that a killer whale or "one of them giant squids" was waiting for them. You can well imagine their shock at what greeted them that day on the beach. There, sitting tangled in a mess of seaweed, was a gigantic baby boy. Some reckon he was more than "three fathoms long" – that's sea talk for eighteen feet tall. When he set to wailing, the folk all swore they heard the Nantucket foghorn sounding.

No one knew the baby boy's background, but some folk say that Alfred Bulltop Stormalong, as he was named right then and there, surely had the sea in his blood. Talk was that he descended from a line of great seafaring folk, and his family tree included the likes of Odysseus, the great Greek sea adventurer, and old Noah himself.

Young Stormalong was taken in by a kindly old couple who turned their dory into a cradle for him. The townsfolk described him as a happy baby, who cut his first teeth gnawing on a whale-bone and who grew in leaps and bounds from his nighttime bottles of Cape Cod clam chowder. When he'd cry for more, ships ten miles offshore would wonder why the foghorn was blaring so loudly on a clear night.

"Little" Stormalong, or "Stormy" as he was affectionately known, grew bigger by the day, if not by the hour. By the time he went to school, he was close to five whole fathoms tall. Every day after classes he raced down to the beach, where he liked to dig in the sand. Village children were warned to stay away from the sandcastles he built, as one poor little fellow "near drowned" in the moat. His father had to dive in, saving him in the nick of time. Parents also warned their children not to follow Stormy when he went swimming, as it was nothing for that boy to swim out to sea for an entire afternoon of play with the whales off Martha's Vineyard.

When he turned twelve, it was clear Stormy no longer fit in with his playmates. This was not because they did not like him. Truth was they loved their giant pal with the big heart and the warm smile. But Stormy had outgrown the schoolhouse and most of the small Cape Cod houses. He was now a full six fathoms in height, which is thirty-six feet tall.

Stormy knew it was time to see the big wide world, so he packed his bags and left for the city of Boston, where he had heard everything was bigger and grander. Of course that proved to be yet another Cape Cod yarn, for Boston houses were sometimes even smaller than those on the cape. Stormy figured the only place he'd ever fit in was out in the big blue sea. This being the Golden Age of Sail, he set off to the docks and signed up as a cabin boy aboard the *Lady of the Sea*, a stately clipper trade ship bound for the China seas.

The whole ship listed to starboard when Stormalong stepped on deck, and the skipper had to hold on to the rail for dear life, so as not to be pitched right into the sea. With another step, the boat righted itself in the water and Stormalong knew he had found his sea legs. The captain soon saw that his cabin boy was a great addition aboard ship. Why, sailors no longer had to climb the masts. Stormalong could reach right up the mainmast to straighten out a flapping sail. That boy could unknot a rope "same as if he was untying a shoelace." He soon became first mate and another cabin boy was hired. Toby was an orphan the same age as Stormalong. The two got along swimmingly – that's sea talk for just swell – and went on to become lifelong pals. So they didn't have to shout at each other to be heard, Stormalong often carried Toby in his pocket.

One day Stormalong showed Toby how far he could throw a harpoon. He hurled his sailor's cap far out into the water, then pitched the harpoon, spearing his hat and pulling it back to the deck. "Do it again," Toby cried in excitement, "and make it go out even farther this time." On the tenth time, Stormalong threw the harpoon over sixty fathoms out to sea, but it did not spear the cap. It landed with a thud and settled deep into the back of a humpback whale. Water spouted high into the air and the whale bolted. Stormalong hung on to the line attached to the harpoon for dear life; Toby hung on to the lining of his friend's pea jacket;

the rest of the crew held on to their hats while the *Lady of the Sea* was taken on the ride of her life.

The whale heaved and twisted, dove and pulled, trying to free itself from the line. Stormalong would not let go and the whale plowed straight through fifty-foot Atlantic waves, twisted "sharp south" along the coast of South America, then zigzagged over to Africa and back to cross through the Strait of Magellan. Finally, Stormalong jumped ship and landed atop the whale's humped back. He rode that whale like it was a rodeo bronco and brought that Nantucket sleigh ride, as many have called it, to a close.

Well, that's just one whale of a tale that folk still tell. Then there was the time Stormalong got "into a tussle" with a giant octopus. It all started one fine summer day when the *Lady of the Sea* was anchored in deep ocean off the West Indies, while the crew made some much-needed repairs. By now, Stormalong had become a boatswain, or bosun as the crew all called it, which meant he was officially in charge of sails, riggings, and the workings of the anchor.

One day, when the order was given for the anchor to be hoisted, the command was obeyed but nothing moved. The capstan bar that pulled up the anchor's chain could not be budged in the slightest. The anchor stayed moored on the ocean floor. Even Stormalong's strength made no difference to the situation. He peered down into the deep green sea, then told the crew the only thing to do was for him to dive down and get a firsthand look at that "ornery anchor." Everyone figured it would be a simple matter. No doubt the anchor had gotten hooked around some coral reef.

The crew stood back, holding on to masts and ropes so as not to be knocked overboard as Stormalong's enormous splash rocked the boat. Then, they looked over the side into the deep green. Stormalong was out of sight below the surface and the crew figured he'd quickly return with the anchor. He had told them not to worry when he dove deep, as he could hold his breath underwater for weeks, if need be. But the crew looked concerned as minutes, then half an hour, then more than an hour rolled by with no sign of Stormalong.

Something major was going on down in the salty depths, for the ocean water was slapping hard against the *Lady of the Sea* and rocking her furiously back and forth and up and down. Strange crashes came from under the churning sea – the sound of gun battle followed by what sounded like a whip. Black slimy liquid surfaced, then the water stirred up like bathwater going down the drain. The crew knew this was no ordinary coral reef causing the fracas and they worried for the safety of their trusty friend, Stormalong. "What could be causing such great thrashing?" they wondered. Some guessed earthquake; others reckoned it had to be an erupting underwater volcano.

Well, the truth of what was happening when he got to the bottom of things goes something like this. There, clinging on to the anchor like nobody's business, was a giant octopus. Now Stormalong knew this was troublesome all round. If he didn't loosen its grip on the anchor, his ship was going nowhere in a hurry. But if that "great black sea varmint" got loose, it would be fast on the prowl looking for lunch up on deck. Stormalong knew the crew was easy pickings for this slimy creature and his eight suction-cupped tentacles.

So being a mannerly sort, Stormalong felt he should give the critter a chance to resolve things in a civil manner. "'Scuse me, Mister Giant Octopus, sir," the kindly bosun said. Clearing his throat he continued, "I would be mighty obliged if you'd lift your tentacles from my anchor." Well, that "slimy critter" didn't bat an eyelash and hung on even tighter. That was the end of Stormalong's politeness and patience in the matter.

As Stormalong later told it, "I held on hard with one hand to a long wriggly arm and, with my other hand, I pried each of his suckers off the anchor. They made a loud sound like popguns going off. Then I moved to the next arm and before I knew it, the freed one was right back on. Now I realized the fighting wouldn't be easy. So I teased that varmint, calling him names like 'sucker boy' and 'eight arms.' And he got good and miffed at me, he did, and his tentacles came whipping out as he tried to lasso me in for the kill. I avoided him for the good part of an hour, then he nabbed me and hauled me in. That's when I knew I would have to play tough. Soon as I was close in, I moved my hand up under one of his tentacle pits and I tickled that critter for dear life. He shouted

'Stop it,' but I tickled him mercilessly until black tears oozed from his eyes and his arms went limp with exhaustion. Then I grabbed all eight tentacles, tied them in giant knots, and kicked that varmint like a football headed straight for Antarctica."

When the sea calmed and Stormalong surfaced, the crew marvelled at their bosun's bravery. They gave him a round of cheers, but all Stormalong had to say for himself was "'Tweren't nothin' now, fellows, just a good wrassling match with a two-ton octopus. That's all."

After Stormalong ate a small meal of two dozen sea pies, a pot of fish stew, and six pans of salty dog biscuits, he retired for a well-deserved nap. The crew hauled in the anchor and sang their tired crewmate a capstan chantey for a lullaby. They made up words about their dear old bosun, Mister Stormalong. It's a chantey that is still sung on the high seas, only sailors eventually had to add one more verse:

O Stormy's dead and gone to rest,
To my way, you storm along,
Of all the sailors he was best.
Ay, ay, ay, Mister Stormalong.

WHY THE SEA IS SALT

Once upon a time, in a village far over the sea, there lived two brothers. One brother was wealthy and the other lived in extreme poverty. Many times the poor one had to ask the rich one for help, so it came as no surprise to the rich man when his brother came knocking yet again late one Christmas Eve.

HAVING BEEN WARNED NOT TO CALL ON HIS prior visit, the poor man fell quickly to his knees and pleaded, "Dear brother, in the name of heaven and all that is good, I pray you help me. My wife and I have no food, nary a morsel, and we shall go hungry this Christmas. Please, spare us even a cup of flour, that we may have something for Christmas dinner."

While the wealthy brother may have been rich in money, in truth he was extremely poor of spirit. He was a miser, who took no pleasure in helping others. "Ahh! I will help you this one last time, but you must make me a promise."

"Anything, anything; only please spare some food," cried the poor brother.

The rich man smiled and continued slowly, just to taunt his desperate brother, "Go then to the smokehouse and get yourself a fat bacon." Then he added nastily, "When you leave my house this time, go straight to the devil and never ever come back here to ask for anything again!"

The poor brother ran to the smokehouse, unhooked a large fatty side of bacon, and ran from the premises. He started down a forest path on his way to find the devil, for he was a man of his word. He hadn't gone far when a wizened old man appeared from behind a clump of bushes. The brother bade him a good evening and the mysterious fellow asked him where he was headed with the flitch of bacon. The brother wasted not a word: "I'm going straight to the devil if I only knew where to find him."

"Well," smiled the old man, "you're on the right path. Just up ahead, beyond that copse, you'll see a house in the shadows of the oak tree. Go bravely to the door and knock. You'll be let in by impish-looking creatures. Only don't be fooled, for they are the devil's helpers; but here is how to trick them."

The poor brother listened intently to the strange instructions. "When you finally get inside," the old man said, "they'll pester the living daylights out of you for that flitch of bacon, for they do love smoky meat. But mind my words. Do not sell it to them unless they give you their quern. It stands behind the door."

The brother thought this an unusual barter. "A quern, did you say?"

"Yes," said the old man. "'Tis an old grinding mill they keep behind the door. But, you see, it is not just any quern – it has magical properties. When you have secured the magic mill, bring it back and I will show you how it works."

The poor brother thanked the old man and headed off. Just as he had been warned, a horde of devilish imps with long drooping noses met him at the door, all of them cackling and cursing evil spells. They drooled and grabbed, then haggled for the bacon.

Sure enough, the quern was sitting behind the door. A bargain was quickly struck and, as the devil's imps tore at the flitch, the poor brother left with the quern. He couldn't help but wonder if such an ordinary-looking object was worth his Christmas dinner. Nonetheless, he hurried back to the spot in the forest where he had met the old man.

"Now give it here, and I'll teach you the magic," the old man said, "for this quern can grind out anything you ask of it. Anything, my good man. The trick is in starting, then stopping it. To start say 'Grind, mill, grind,' but listen carefully for it is the stopping of the mill that is the true trick." The wizened man placed the magic mill on its side and said, "It will only stop when resting in this position, then say 'Grind no more, mill,' and it will be done. Then you may store it – away from curious eyes is best."

Again the poor brother thanked the old man, and headed home to show the miraculous mill to his wife. She was pacing in the cold of their cottage kitchen. All day she had waited, with no firewood to light. When her husband entered with an old grinding mill and no food, she burst into tears. "I have waited all day for this," she wailed. "For heaven's sake explain why you have come home with nothing for Christmas dinner."

Her husband set the quern on the table. "Now I shall grind out the meal of your dreams," he said. She watched in fascination, for as soon as he had spoken the words "Grind, mill, grind. Grind us a Christmas dinner with all the trimmings," the quern handle started to turn on its own and from the top of the mill came sweet potato pie, cranberry sauce, a roasted goose, and plum pudding. Next came two lit candles, napkins, wine and glasses, and *poof* – a fire in the hearth to make things merry. "Upon my word" was all his happy wife could say. Seeing her contentment, the husband laid the mill on its side and spoke the command, "Grind no more, mill." And the mill stopped its grinding.

Over the holidays the man and his wife decided to entertain all of their friends and they invited the rich brother to their cottage. He was perplexed at his poor brother's sudden turn of fortune and asked, "Tell me how it is that on Christmas Eve you had 'nary a morsel,' and now suddenly there seems to be no limit to your larder." The poor brother had no intention of showing him the quern, but as the night wore on, the rich brother became more and more insistent. Finally, when all the neighbors had departed, the poor brother brought out the quern to show his brother.

"I have always helped you," began the greedy rich brother. "I therefore think it only fair if you allow me to have this quern." Again, after many objections, the kinder brother relented and a bargain was struck: the poor brother would keep the quern until after harvest, then sell it to his brother for three hundred dollars.

The poor brother made good use of his time with the quern and set in enough supplies to last for years. He was used to living in poverty and this amount of wealth and ease seemed more than enough. At the end of harvest, the rich brother came by for the quern, giving his brother three hundred dollars. After he was shown how to start it up, he made his excuses and left. He hurried home before his brother could stop him, but in so doing he failed to learn the secret of how to stop the mill.

The next morning, the rich brother brought out the quern. He told his wife and his servants that they should go out for the day, for he would have a wonderful feast ready for them when they returned. When they left, he thought of all he would prepare with the quern. "Grind, mill, grind," he began. "Serve us a thick and hearty soup of herrings and milk."

The mill immediately began to whir and grind. Out came ladlefuls of white fishy soup straight into the pottery bowls on the table. "Stop, mill, stop. That is just fine for starters," said the man. But the mill kept grinding. Soon the tablecloth was a soupy mess and the hot broth spilled over to the floor. "Stop, mill, stop now, I say," said the man, beginning to feel frantic. The mill quickened its pace.

The soup was up past his ankles now and the man opened his front door. "Enough, enough! Stop now, I command you," he said anxiously, but the broth poured faster and the man was pushed out the door into the yard. The quern sailed on top of the hot milky river while the man ran in front, trying desperately to think of other commands that might stop it from grinding – "Cease! Quit! It is sufficient! Halt! Desist! WHOA!" Nothing worked.

He ran with the scalding broth burning his heels. Townspeople looked on in amazement as he slipped on satiny herring slivers, then skidded across puddles of milk. At last he reached his brother's cottage. "Take back your quern, I beg you. Make it stop before we are all drowned." The poor brother did take back the quern, but not until he had collected another three hundred dollars.

He was happy to have the mill back, for now he thought of all the wondrous changes he could make to his home. Every day his cottage became more spectacular – the mill even ground out gold bricks for the walls. The brother's home gleamed in the sun and could be seen glimmering from far out at sea.

The poor brother's home became the talk of the countryside, and people from far and near came to view it. A sea captain noticed something gold and glistening in the moonlight one night, and made for port just to see what had caught his eye from the water. As he walked toward the resplendent cottage, the townsfolk told him of the magic mill that could grind out anything that was wished for. "Imagine," thought the sly old captain, "why I could grind out my own salt, rare and tasty salt for the king, and never have to travel through dangerous faraway seas again." He stood in a daydream before the golden cottage, thinking of what great fortune he could amass with possession of the quern.

"Come in," called the poor brother, "and rest your weary bones, my friend." Over a pot of tea, the brother showed the sea captain the mill.

"Pray tell me how it works," beseeched the curious captain. The brother told him the magic words to get it to grind. The two men talked and by the end of the evening, the brother invited the captain to take lodging for the night. This is just what the captain had hoped would be the case, for in the middle of the night when the whole house was silent and all in the village slept, the captain stole the quern and ran to his ship. He quietly set sail under the full moon and stopped only at the crack of dawn, when he was safely far out to sea.

He set the quern in the ship's hold and commanded: "Grind, mill, grind. Fill my ship with the finest of salt." Not a moment passed before white salt was spraying from the mill. The ship's hold filled to the brim and the captain picked up the mill and told it to stop. Still it spilled over. He set it down on the deck and commanded it to cease grinding. But the deck soon looked like a white sandy beach. There were mounds of glistening salt all over the deck, burying the steering wheel and climbing up the masts.

The captain tried to scoop the salt up, but it sifted through his fingers. "Stop! Stop!" he bellowed as he scampered up to the crow's nest for safety, but the groaning and creaking going on below drowned out his words. By this time, the ship was weighted down by the massive amounts of salt. Still the mill ground on.

At last, with an almighty moan, the ship broke in half from the sheer weight of the salt and sank into the sea. The captain watched as his precious cargo dissolved like sugar. Within a

minute the ship and its captain disappeared deep beneath the surface. But the mill kept on grinding.

To this very day, the magic quern lies on the ocean floor, forever grinding out its last command. And that is why the sea is salt.

THE WORLD SHIP

LONG AGO WHEN FOLK STILL BELIEVED THE earth was flat, someone advanced a rather curious theory about the real workings of this planet. What if Mother Earth was really a big ship? "Just suppose," someone imagined, "if what we thought were mountains were really giant masts and the land we walked over was the main deck." And so, over time, these enormous myths were whittled down in the tellings to mere tall tales.

This world ship was so big that sailors who started climbing to the crow's nest as teenage lads came down with long white hair and beards. Great teams of workhorses were needed to carry crew members from stem to stern. If they left by dawn, a good gallop would have them there by moonrise the next week.

French sailors told tall tales of another gigantic ship they called *Chasse Foudre*, which means "Lightning Chaser." She was so enormous, she was seven full years in tacking, for her mainmast alone was larger than all of Europe, taking a whole forest of trees to make. The multicolored streamer high atop the mast was nothing short of a real-for-goodness rainbow.

In his later years, Mister Stormalong had a giant ship of similar proportions to the *Chasse Foudre*. The *Tuscarora* was her name.

One of the biggest problems for a ship at that great height was getting stuck in the clouds, or hit by the point of a crescent moon. The topmasts were hinged so they didn't knock stars out of their constellations, and the very tips of the masts were padded so as not to poke holes in the sky itself. But perhaps such occurrences are commonplace when a tale gets to be this tall!

THE TSAR OF THE SEA

Down in the very deeps of the Russian sea lived a water king, a northern Neptune whose royal title was the Tsar of the Sea. Stories have been told of this bold and laughing Tsar. Some sailors said he appeared to them at sea; others said the mighty Tsar could shape-shift and move in water form to appear in any river or lake in Russia. Though many claimed to have seen him, only one human had the privilege of entertaining the Tsar. For all his bluster and sea strength, the Tsar was a spirit who loved good music and an opportunity to dance. And when he danced, the very ocean churned. This is the story of how a man named Sadko came to play music for the Tsar of the Sea.

L ONG AGO IN RUSSIA, IN THE CITY OF NOVGOROD, a poor man named Sadko played music for his supper. He played upon a *gusli*, an instrument much like a little lap harp, which his father had made out of maple wood. The father was poor and the gusli was all he had to leave his son when he died. It was not worth much money, but in the talented hands of Sadko, it made exquisite music. Folk asked Sadko to play for feasts and weddings, tossing kopecks into his cap as they waltzed to his sweet music. Still the musician made barely enough to have even the most frugal existence.

Sadko's greatest pleasure came at day's end, when he sat alone in the quietness along the banks of Lake Ilmen, just outside the city. Here he played the songs his heart sang. He listened to the lapping waters and composed melodies on his gusli for the little lake waves to dance to. As he played, he thought he heard gleeful laughter, high-pitched and rippling like watery melodies. He stopped and looked into the water, where a full moon shone. Glimpsing a long line of dancing maidens, he wondered if these were the Rusalkas – the lake spirits in the fairy tales he had heard as a young boy. In an instant they faded and then, in the center of the reflected moon, there appeared the most beautiful face Sadko had ever seen. It was that of a young woman with long golden hair, wearing a tiara of silver and seashells. Her eyes were as azure as a summer sea, her face as white as pearls. Then she smiled and the water rippled with giggles. "We have been dancing, young musician," she said. "Your music has entertained us in our underwater palace halls. Our father, the mighty Tsar of the Sea, is well pleased and wishes to meet the human who can play such songs. Play on, good musician, and our father will rise from the lake to meet you."

Sadko watched as the beautiful face disappeared into the glimmering moonlit waters. He picked up his gusli and played a bold and stately song, for it was not every day one met royalty, even if this tsar did come from under the sea. As the music grew faster, the waters far out in the lake began to churn. Large waves splashed around the rocks where Sadko sat, and up came the greatest figure he had ever seen.

The burly tsar made giant strides through the lake toward Sadko. The water glistened in his long green hair and dripped from his wild beard of kelp and seaweed. He wore a crown of ocean gold, with huge chunks of amber embedded in it. The tsar threw back his head and, in a voice as mighty as the ocean itself, he let out a generous laugh. "Good Sadko, musician of Novgorod," he began, "your music has charmed all in my underwater kingdom. We have danced and sung along to your melodies. Never has there been such merrymaking beneath the waves. For this, I am most pleased. My thirteen daughters and I wish to give you a gift of thanks, for your music has given us much pleasure."

Sadko knew he was in the presence of greatness and could not find the words to speak. Instead he played a gentle melody on his gusli. The Tsar of the Sea laughed another boisterous laugh and the waves leaped, then calmed as he spoke: "Ah, dear Sadko. I know you struggle to make a living. But I guarantee when you cast your net into the waters tomorrow, and from thereon in, you will have greater wealth than you could ever dream possible. This is our gift to you for your gift of music." At this the tsar sank beneath the waters and the whole lake became perfectly still.

The next morning Sadko hurried to the lake with his gusli under his arm and his fishing net slung over his shoulder. He cast the net into the lake and thought of the tsar's words. "Do I dare dream of such wealth? Yes, it has been promised," he told himself. He hauled in the net and there were ocean treasures more beautiful than any sea chest might hold. He pulled out gold pieces the size of codfish, and opened oyster shells to behold luminescent pearls. The beauty of the catch was a feast for his eyes, for the shining red, blue, green, and gold were perfectly shaped rubies, sapphires, emeralds, and amber. Silver and gold coins from sunken treasure shone in the dazzling sea mix. Sadko packed up his net with his sea fortune and sat down on the bank to play a song of thanks to the tsar. The waters rippled and Sadko thought he heard a choir of distant voices singing to his music.

The next day Sadko returned and, when he pulled in his net, he had doubled his fortune. Again, he played a song of gratitude to the tsar for his blessing. Each day the pile of treasures grew and Sadko returned to Novgorod an extremely wealthy man.

Immediately he bought twelve of the largest and finest ships in port, manned all vessels, and set sail across the sea to make even greater fortune as a merchant. At the return of his first trip, he built a mansion in the city and asked the fair maiden Lubasha to be his wife. They would marry when he returned again from sea. This next trip was to be over many of the world's oceans and to last for as many years, but Lubasha said indeed she would wait for Sadko to return.

After several years of travel and good fortune at every turn, Sadko became accustomed to living with constant great wealth. In fact, he had come to expect it. Often at nightfall he felt tired and full from the cook's hearty meals and servings of the best vodka. Where once he had ended the day by playing his gusli out to the waters for the Tsar of the Sea, he now could not be bothered to make the short trip up to the deck. He slowly forgot this nightly ritual and his music-making altogether. His gusli hung silent on his cabin wall.

Then one day, when the wind was brisk, Sadko's ship came to a complete standstill. Other vessels passed with the wind in their sails, but Sadko and his crew sat becalmed. The sails of the great ship fell slack, while all about them the sea sat calm. The boat did not even bob in the water. It was as if a great hand held the ship tightly in place and the wind was holding its breath.

The sailors looked about in fright. "Surely this is the doing of the great and mighty Tsar of the Sea," one shouted in panic. "I have heard he is ferocious when angered. One of us has done him wrong." All eyes stared around. Each sailor thought of something he had done that may have brought on the tsar's punishment. "I whistled aboard ship on midnight watch," one confessed. Another added, "No, 'twas I. My wife turned the basin upside down on the very morning we set sail. 'Twas a Friday, no less. Ah, my friends, I should have told you." Yet another piped up, "I'm sure I brought this fate upon the ship for just the morning of our voyage, I stopped to talk to a farmer, and didn't we talk about hares." The whole crew hushed him for using a taboo word shipboard. But what did it matter now, for the tsar was already angered.

All this time Sadko hung his head. He knew in his heart what had brought on the sea tsar's wrath. He hurried to his cabin and returned to the deck with his gusli. "My good men," began the fair and honest merchant, "I am who the tsar wants. For I have the tsar to thank for my good fortune all these years, and in my comfort I have forgotten to pay him proper tribute for a long time now." Before his men could stop him, Sadko, with his gusli tucked under his arm, jumped overboard into the deep blue of the Caspian Sea.

For a while, Sadko stayed afloat holding on to his gusli. Then, as his men watched in horror, a great green hand surfaced, grabbing Sadko tightly in its clutches. The brave captain was pulled down through the sea while his men prayed for his soul.

At first Sadko held his breath, fearing he would drown. But when he finally gasped for air, he was amazed to find the water around him was like the air. Deeper he sank until he came to the floor of the ocean. There in front of him was a magnificent white coral palace, with sea-green columns studded with mother-of-pearl. Every window and door was trimmed with gold. He walked through gardens of sea ferns and splendid coral spreads. At each side of the palace door, giant fish with silver helmets stood guard. They opened the doors and lead him into the royal chamber of the Tsar of the Sea.

Inside was even more spectacular. The giant hall shone with polished stones, jewels, and more silver and gold – treasures from wrecked ships that had sunk to the seabed centuries before. There on a glistening crystal throne was the tsar, looking fierce and tormented by Sadko's presence. "You," he thundered, "how dare you forget the source of your wealth." Sadko knew the truth in the tsar's words and hung his head in shame. The tsar was moved and in a slightly gentler tone, he went on, "How sad, too, that you have forgotten so precious a musical gift. . . ."

In an abrupt change of tone, the tsar suddenly roared: "I command you, Sadko, to play like you have never played before. We have waited for your sweet sea songs for too long. Play now."

Sadko raised his gusli and immediately played. Underwater, the melodies seemed sweeter, and the sounds of the strings echoed everywhere through the massive crystal hall. The tsar sighed with pleasure and tapped his great scaly fingers gently to the beat of the sea melody. When the song ended, the tsar spoke up: "Good Sadko, I wish to always hear your music. I wish you to always live here under the sea. My daughters are all so fond of you that any one of them would be pleased to marry you. Please pick one of my daughters as your wife and you shall live happily in my sea palace."

Sadko dared not refuse the tsar's hospitality, for he had seen the power of his anger. Although he loved Lubasha with his whole heart, he saw no choice but to pick a sea bride. The tsar's thirteen daughters floated past in their feathery white gowns. They looked as graceful as swans, for indeed that is how they often appeared above on the waters. Sadko found each to be beautiful and seemingly of a sweet nature. He could not choose until the last sea princess appeared. "Where have I seen this golden-haired beauty before?" he wondered. Then he remembered the water maiden who appeared in the lake many years before. He would marry her.

"Let the celebration begin, for Sadko will marry the princess Volkova," announced the tsar, and he commanded Sadko to play his best dance music. The whole court erupted into a great swirl of merriment. All about, the sea creatures began to twirl and dive to the music, swimming in and around the assembled court. The princesses danced in a circle around their sister Volkova and the tsar, who had at first been clapping his hands, started to tap his giant toes on the ocean floor.

Sadko watched a young sea horse leaping about to the music with so much glee that the little fellow soared straight up through the castle turret. Sadko could see through the sea-glass roof and kept his eyes on the spritely sea horse as it neared the surface. There he saw a terrible sight, for the surface of the sea above him was wild and stormy. Ships were sinking from the giant crashing waves, while others struck rocks. The whole sea was in chaos from the dancing below. Terrified his own crews would be drowned, Sadko stopped playing and broke every string on the gusli.

The dancing came to an abrupt halt and the great sea tsar glared. "I have no more use for you," he said. "I am only happy you did not marry my daughter. Sadko, be off with you." And at that, Sadko found himself rising quickly to the surface. His crewmen, finally able to catch a breath after the raging seas calmed down, spotted their captain floating in the water. They plucked him out of the sea and sailed back toward Novgorod.

A full twelve years had passed since Sadko had seen Lubasha, but when they met each other again they knew they would always be happy together. Sadko most willingly promised his new bride never to sail the seas again. They moved into their mansion, but spent much time at their small cottage by Lake Ilmen. There, on moonlit nights, the couple went down to the water's edge, where Sadko played beautiful melodies once again on his gusli.

Late one evening they thought they heard rippling laughter far out in the water. Sadko remembered and played the song he had composed in the sea princess' honor. Then he listened for the words in the watery ripples – words he alone could decipher: "My heart is brimming with joy at your happiness, dear musician." Again he played.

Volkova was so moved by his music that she followed its sweet strains back to Novgorod, growing on her travels to become the River Volkov. From there she easily streamed into the Caspian Sea.

Deep down below in his great ocean palace, her father, the tsar, was most pleased, for he could hear Sadko's enchanting music above him. All was well for everyone, but every now and again, when the sea swelled and breakers crashed with fury, it was said that the Tsar of the Sea just could not help tapping his giant toes to the beat of Sadko's music.

ODYSSEUS AND THE THREE PERILS

Their song is death and makes destruction please.
– From *The Odyssey* by Alexander Pope

Odysseus was a young man when he set out to fight with the Greeks in the great Trojan War. He had no idea when he left his wife and infant son how long and arduous a voyage he was undertaking. The war with Troy was in itself a nine-year battle. He left Troy in triumph, but his journey home to Ithaca was anything but easy, getting off to an ill-fated start when Odysseus enraged the supreme deity of the sea.

O DYSSEUS AND HIS TIRED AND WEARY CREW took refuge from wind and storm on what appeared to be a small and peaceful island. But the inhabitant of that island was none other than the cyclops

Polyphemus. The one-eyed giant was the son of Poseidon, god of the sea. Immediately, he captured the entire crew and held them captive in his cave. Each morning and evening, the cyclops bent down and plucked up two men for his meal. The rest of the crew could only watch helplessly as the monster held them tightly in his clutches. Then he shook, tore at, and finally ate the poor souls. The gruesome giant, his hunger satisfied for the moment, fell into a deep sleep. Several of the crew perished in this ghastly manner.

Odysseus was determined to escape and searched the cave for any semblance of a weapon. There it was – the cyclops' giant club. It took several men to move the massive piece of wood, and all night they worked to whittle down the end into a sharp point. Near dawn, they put the tip into the burning embers of the giant's fire and, when the point was red-hot, they picked up the pole aiming the burnt end straight for the cyclops' eye. They drove it in with all their might.

The cyclops awoke screaming in pain as he wrestled to remove the stick, which had pierced his eye and blinded him. While he struggled, the crew ran swiftly down the cliffside to their ship. They looked up as they rowed away. Polyphemus, wild in his rage, had ripped huge pieces of rock from the mountain, hurling them off the cliff edge in hopes of sinking the escaping ship. In absolute fury, he screamed his curses at the crew and called out to his father, Poseidon, to bring revenge on Odysseus.

From that point on, Odysseus was to encounter perils, each horrific and deathly. The voyage would take him eleven years, at a terrible cost. He would lose every one of his crewmen and his ship. He was to learn of the power of the curse at one of their first landfalls – a mysterious island where the powerful enchantress, Circe, dwelt. Odysseus knew of her magics and did not fall prey to her sorcery, as all had before him. Far from being angered, Circe showed favor to Odysseus. She escorted the sailor and his crew to a large banquet table laden with fruit and bread, honey and wine. "Clever and brave Odysseus," said Circe, "you and your men have journeyed long." She gestured for them to sit at the table. "As honored guests of my island, I invite you to feast and relax, for many are the dangers that await you upon your departure."

Her warnings were stern and Circe commanded the attention of all at the table. She foretold of three immediate perils that would require every ounce of strength and courage they could muster. "First," warned the enchantress, "come the sirens. Beware of what appear to be their charms, for many a mariner has fallen under their sea spell. The sirens' voices are most sweet. Passing ships are bewitched by the gentle waves of unearthly melody surrounding them." Circe paused, then in hushed tones added, "But their music is poison and pulls sailors from their senses. Many have strained to hear more clearly the splendor of their music, only to abandon ship and follow the tones across the waters where the sirens sit."

Now Circe looked directly at each and every crewman. "You must know that the sirens never pursue; they merely wait," she warned. "And, oh, how lovely they appear with their outstretched arms beckoning wave-weary sailors to swim that short distance to their white sandy island. But all this, my friends, is illusion." Her face hardened and her eyes flashed wildly. "Alas! The poor wretch who abandons his senses and follows that music swims to his death. For the beach is not made white from gleaming sand. In truth, it is strewn with the bleached limbs, bones, and skulls of those who perished before. And when a new victim swims ashore, the sirens can only gloat. For these beautiful maidens are really bird women. They swoop down on their prey, then holding him in their talons, they shred and tear at him until he becomes just one more pile of bones. Remember, so insistent is their call that whole crews have dived into the waves, leaving their unguided ships to wreck on a rocky shore."

Odysseus and his men looked stunned. Surely this was a greater peril than even the cyclops. "Pray tell us, wise Circe," begged Odysseus, "do you know a way for us to make safe passage through such enticement?"

Circe smiled, for her powers as a sorceress had made her an equal to any dark and wretched form of enchantment. "Here is what you must do, but mind you follow my instructions exactly. As you near the Isle of the Sirens – and you will know for always there is a dead calm before they sing – all of you must soften the beeswax that I will give you and plug your ears with it." She continued, "Odysseus, I fear that your curiosity will be the ruin of you. Should you desire to hear their songs, you can only safely do so by having your crew bind you hand and foot to the mast." At this, she stared at the crewmen and said, "Remember, he will beg and plead to be set free. He will order you to obey him, but you must not. If he struggles with his bindings, lash him even tighter to the mast, or all is lost."

Odysseus, weary with the thought of what further dangers could lie in store, asked Circe to impart whatever other helpful knowledge and secrets she possessed. And the sorceress told Odysseus and his men of the Wandering Rocks, two great jutting sea rocks that roamed free of the ocean floor. They were to be avoided, for to pass between them was certain destruction. The Wandering Rocks would crash together, smashing any ship into splinters.

Then Circe beckoned Odysseus to walk with her. She spoke in whispers for a long time, obviously about the third peril. The crew wondered what could be more deadly than meeting up with the cyclops, sirens, and crashing rocks. But they dared not ask for they could not bear to hear. They trusted Odysseus to lead them out of harm's way.

The next morning, the enchantress gave Odysseus a ball of pliable beeswax. Standing on the beach, she waved her hand and a sea wind rose up to send the ship on its way at a good pace. Odysseus and his crew had not been long at sea when the wind suddenly died down and the ship's sails hung slack. They sat on a becalmed sea in the heat of the noonday sun; all about was an eerie stillness. Remembering Circe's warning, Odysseus acted with haste. He held the beeswax up to the sun and ordered his men to take enough of the softened wax to plug their ears, for all knew the deathly music was about to start. No one needed reminding of what was to be done next. Odysseus went willingly to the mast, where he was lashed tightly into place. Then, in the heat and stillness, the men rowed with all their might.

Sure enough, off in the distance appeared a glorious shining white beach island. It looked to be an inviting paradise, for there sat the most beautiful maidens with their arms held out toward the ship. The rowers bent their heads and pulled hard on the oars. Odysseus was the only one to experience the full power of the sirens' enchantment. The maidens raised their eyes and gazed straight into his. Then came their song. It began faintly – a sweet and beckoning sound. The irresistible chant was at first mesmerizing. Slowly it grew louder, then ever more insistent, until it seemed to fill the very air Odysseus breathed.

Part of the spell was that those who heard the sirens' song heard the words they most longed to hear. For Odysseus, the choir of sirens sang of his great heroic deeds, praising him and promising him even greater fame and success.

Come to us, Odysseus,
Most famed of all Greek warriors.

You alone are the pride and glory of all of Greece.
Rest for a time, tired Odysseus,
For you deserve it.

Again they fixed their stares, trying to coax the now half-mad hero. And again they sang songs proclaiming him to be the chosen one.

Blessed are you, mighty Odysseus,
For you have heard our voice –
The sweet song of secrets
Only the wise may know.
Follow the beauty, Odysseus.

Odysseus strained to follow the music. With every muscle tensed, he twisted and struggled to loosen his bindings. He pleaded with his crew, forgetting they could not hear him. He yelled orders to be untied, promising he would not abandon ship for the sirens. Two of the crew, seeing his desperation, moved forward and tightened his bonds. Then returning to the rowing bench, they set a faster pace. They knew the spell must be powerful, for Odysseus was a sailor who had already experienced remarkable encounters and enchantments. None had so transfixed him.

As they rowed past the island, one man dared look out. He knew Odysseus was enraptured with visions of sparkling white sands. But without the music to enchant, the rower saw an island littered and piled high with the skeletal remains of once bold mariners. He also saw the murderous coldness in the sirens' fixed glances, knowing Odysseus saw only beauty. As the wretched island disappeared on the horizon, he looked to Odysseus. Once more there was reason in Odysseus' face. The crewmen cut him loose from the mast, removing the wax plugs from their own ears.

"I thank you for remaining steadfast, my friends," Odysseus said as he further regained his senses, "for their insidious cries sounded like the sweetest melodies, and I yearned to follow their call. I cannot describe the disgust I feel at being rendered so mad by their enchantments."

The spell and their spirits had lifted. A breeze was picking up and soon filled the sails. The crewmen had felt unbelievable relief at having safely passed the sirens. They had put the fact that it was merely the first of Circe's perils out of their minds. But the optimism was quickly broken by a loud crashing sound. The crash and the deafening ocean roar that followed could mean only one thing: they were sailing toward the second peril, the Wandering Rocks. Since the rocks and their surrounding reefs were not rooted to the ocean floor, the ship was on an ever-changing but certain collision course. The sea churned as the tall rocks drifted closer, parted company, then crashed together crushing a gull passing between them.

Odysseus knew he must change course immediately. His heart sank for ahead in the narrow passage was the third of the perils, and he was the only one who knew how truly horrific this obstacle would be. But there was no choice in the matter, for to sail elsewhere guaranteed his ship would be pulverized in an instant.

The crewmen startled when they heard yet another frightening sea sound. They looked to find the passage ahead churning like a giant funnel, with water spraying all about it. "Charybdis," said Odysseus bluntly, "a whirlpool that drinks down the sea and all that passes over it. We must sail well out of her way. Row more to the right side of the strait." Poor Odysseus was sick with upset. He could not tell his men all that Circe had conveyed to him. He could not reveal that six of them were about to meet a gruesome end in the clutches of the monstrous Scylla.

Odysseus knew he must follow Circe's advice. She had told him: "There is no other way than to go through the passage. You must run on Scylla to avoid Charybdis." The men rowed with all their might, going against the strong currents that drew their ship toward the whirlpool. In their struggle to stay away from Charybdis, they came too close to the right side. Out from her cave sprang Scylla. She lurched forward with her six ugly heads, all with wide-open jaws. She snapped them shut bringing in a haul of half a dozen crewmen. As had happened before with the cyclops, there was nothing anyone could do to save the poor men. Odysseus gave the heartless order to keep on rowing and stay on course.

The saddened crew headed on. How hideous this journey had been. Odysseus shuddered when he thought how easy it would have been to follow the sirens. He could only hope there was truth in what Circe had told them: "An oracle condemned the sirens to die should any man pass without succumbing to their song." With the loss of six crewmates to Scylla, Odysseus told the remaining men to take some small measure of comfort in the belief they had put an end to at least one of the three perils. They were worn and weary in every respect, but they had passed the three perils and thought perhaps it would be clear sailing from that point on.

But the wrath and fury of the unforgiving Poseidon was fierce. More misery awaited them on the horizon. The crew sailed forward on their ill-starred voyage. . . .

V

BLOODY
BROADSIDES:
PIRATES!

UNDER THE BLACK FLAG

The Jolly Roger, that sinister black flag with the white skull and crossbones, was a brazen pirate emblem.

THE FIRST PIRATE FLAGS HAD BEEN RED IN color; in fact, the term "Jolly Roger" most likely came from what the French wryly dubbed the hideous flag: *jolie rouge* (pretty red). Others guess the name came from a nickname for the devil: "Old Roger." Whatever its origin, the meaning of the Jolly Roger was all too clear – pirate terror on the high seas and little chance of mercy.

For pirates, the flag was a symbol of brotherhood and solidarity. Perhaps flying it was a rogue's way of laughing death in the face. Most pirates flew black flags, called black jacks, and captains created their own designs to identify their particular brand of terror. They used an array of deathly images, each with a gruesome meaning: a spear indicated violent death, while a bleeding heart meant a slow and torturous death; an hourglass signified that time was running out and a smiling devil face denoted disgrace and torture. It was the Golden Age of Piracy and each black flag inspired panic.

Black flags of legendary pirate captains:

Bartholomew Roberts – The stylish sea captain, also known as Black Bart, sported a black jack with a captain drinking a toast with a skeleton. He also designed a second flag, which flew as a visible vow of revenge. It showed a captain, meant to be Roberts, standing on two skulls labelled ABH and AMH. Black Bart hated the islands of Barbados and Martinique for their actions against him – ABH stood for "A Barbadian's Head"; AMH, "A Martinican's Head." Roberts made good on part of his vow when he hanged the governor of Martinique from the yardarm. When Roberts died, it was said so did the Golden Age of Piracy.

Jack Rackham – Rackham was a dashing pirate, nicknamed Calico Jack because of the bright calico clothing he always wore. His flag design was sobering in comparison to his dress: a skull and two crossed cutlasses instead of bones. Although his message was menacing, Rackham was more cunning than he was brave. Rumor had it he had been thrown off a buccaneering ship for his cowardly ways before becoming a captain. When his pirate ship was attacked by the Royal Navy, Calico Jack hid down in the hold, drinking with his crew. Above on deck, two women pirates – Mary Read and Rackham's wife, Anne Bonney – fought the attackers. Before Calico Jack was hanged, all his wife could say to him was: "Had you fought like a man, you need not have been hanged like a dog!"

Edward Low – The blood-red skeleton on Low's flag instilled true terror, for this pirate captain had a reputation for brutal torture. He had a cruel nature and enjoyed punishing his victims in hideous ways. When one captain threw his ship's treasure into the ocean rather than hand it over to pirates, Low went berserk. He cut off the man's lips and fried them up in front of him. Another time, he cut off a pirate's ears and served them to the poor wretch with salt and pepper.

Thomas Tew – An arm and a knife on a black jack symbolized a grisly end to a victim's life. Tew's flag was a bold variation on this image: a muscular arm holding up a curved Asian sword as a reflection of Tew's pirate territory. He amassed great fortune plundering the rich trading routes of the Indian Ocean. Ironically, Tew was probably slain during battle by a scimitar that looked like the curved sword flying from atop his boat's mainmast.

Edward Teach – Teach, better known as Blackbeard, was a master of drama, never missing an opportunity to fuel his fiendish image. So effective was he that many declared him to be "the devil incarnate." Blackbeard's demonic banner was crammed with ghastly symbols: a horned devil skeleton holding an hourglass in one bony hand, an arrow pointing at a bleeding heart in the other.

GOING ON ACCOUNT

A merry life and a short one shall be my motto.
— Bartholomew Roberts, pirate captain

SIGNING UP TO BE A PIRATE WAS CALLED GOING on account. Those in search of "a merry life," or perhaps just a better life, thought piracy the perfect profession with its promise of adventure, riches, drinking, and gambling. Of course, piracy attracted bullies, cutthroats, and thieves, but many pirates came straight from the navy. To them, pirate life meant freedom from stern and cruel military discipline and appalling work conditions.

No matter how a crewman came to "go on account," every pirate ship had its own rules called Codes of Conduct or Articles of Agreement. They were contracts marking honor among thieves. The crew first elected their captain, then worked as a group to draft the rules. Each pirate signed or marked the document, swearing an oath over a Bible, an ax, or a pair of crossed pistols – a promise to abide by the rules of his ship.

Pirates who stole from fellow crewmen could have their ears and noses slit. Even more dreaded a punishment was Moses' Law, which was a flogging of forty lashes less one. On one ship it was the punishment given for carrying a candle lighted without a lantern. The thirty-nine lashes were administered by a cat-o'-nine-tails, a whip made by unwinding rope and knotting its strands. The pirate being punished most likely had to fashion his own cat-o'-nine-tails. The cords on the knotted end ripped the flesh. Many men passed out or died before the entire thirty-nine lashes were given. Those who survived had to deal with infected wounds.

Death penalties aboard a pirate ship were carried out execution style, with the convicted pirate tied up at the mast and shot. In one gruesome case of murder, the guilty man was bound to his victim and tossed into the sea. But, for pirates, the cruelest sentence was marooning, for their death was guaranteed to be drawn out and torturous. It was a punishment reserved for deserters, murderers, and harsh captains.

The wretched soul was set ashore on a remote island and given one bottle of gunpowder, one bottle of water, one pistol and shot – perhaps a day's grace. The ship then sailed away leaving the convicted man alone to die. The islands were not tropical paradises; often they were little more than sandbars, which at high tide might be completely covered by seawater. There was next to no hope of survival for the castaway. Should he be able to find water and food, his life would be one of barely surviving day to day.

A marooned pirate's one hope of rescue was the appearance of a ship on the horizon. Ironically this could be another death sentence, as a captured pirate was usually tried and hanged. Often the poor wretch came to the conclusion that the best use of his pistol and one shot was to end his misery before it got any worse.

ARTICLES OF AGREEMENT

FROM THE ARTICLES OF AGREEMENT SWORN TO by Bartholomew Roberts' crew:

I. Every man shall have an equal vote in affairs of the moment. He shall have an equal title to the fresh provisions or strong liquors at any time seized, and shall use them at pleasure unless a scarcity may make it necessary for the common good that a retrenchment may be voted.

II. Every man shall be called fairly in turn by the list on board of prizes, because over and above their proper share, they are allowed a shift of clothes. But if they defraud the company to the value of even one dollar in plate, jewels or money, they shall be marooned. If any man rob another he shall have his nose and ears slit, and be put ashore where he shall be sure to encounter hardships.

III. None shall game for money either with dice or cards.

IV. The lights and candles should be put out at eight at night, and if any of the crew desire to drink after that hour they shall sit upon the open deck without lights.

V. Each man shall keep his piece, cutlass and pistols at all times clean and ready for action.

VI. No boy or woman to be allowed. . . .

VII. He that shall desert the ship or his quarters in time of battle shall be punished by death or marooning.

VIII. None shall strike another on board the ship, but every man's quarrel shall be ended on shore by sword or pistol in this manner. At the word of command from the quartermaster, each man being previously placed back to back, shall turn and fire immediately. If any man do not, the quartermaster shall knock the piece out of his hand. If both miss their aim they shall take to their cutlasses, and he that draweth first blood shall be declared the victor.

IX. No man shall talk of breaking up their way of living till each has a share of 1000 pounds. Every man who shall become a cripple or lose a limb in the service shall have 800 pieces of eight from the common stock and for the lesser hurts proportionately.

X. The captain and the quartermaster shall each receive two shares of a prize, the master gunner and boatswain, one and one-half shares, all other officers one and one-quarter, and private gentlemen of fortune one share each.

XI. The musicians shall have rest on the Sabbath Day only by right. On all other days by favour only.

PIRATICAL TALK

Pirates created a world unto themselves, rich with lore, legend, and language. Here are some piratical turns of phrase that became the everyday spoken word under the black flag:

Pirate / Pyrate

The word "pirate" comes from an Ancient Greek word meaning "attack." Pirates were robbers and terrorists on the seas. They could be called by different names depending on which sea they plundered. Corsairs worked the waters of the Barbary Coast, while buccaneers carried out their attacks in the Caribbean. Privateers were legal pirates, having received their country's stamp of approval, a "letter of marque." Pirates were labelled rogues, rovers, sea beggars, freebooters, and filibusters.

Loot, Booty, and Pieces of Eight

Every pirate's dream was to uncover a ship's hold laden with precious gemstones, silver, and gold. Spanish galleons supplied the favored pirate currency – doubloons, which were Spanish gold coins, and pieces of eight: minted silver coins that could, as the name suggests, be cut up into pieces to make change. In 1716, Henry Jennings' pirate ship captured an exciting booty of 350,000 pieces of eight. Among the loot plundered from merchant ships sailing from the East were spices, silks, ivory, porcelain, embroidered cloth, and jewellery.

A well-stocked medicine chest could be treasure as marvellous as gold to a sickly crew. One victim of a pirate attack noted: "No part of the cargo was so much valued by the robbers as the doctor's chest, for they were all poxed to a great degree." Another treasure was capturing a surgeon and forcing him aboard. Weapons were always seized as well as sea charts and navigational equipment, which were highly prized.

Depending on how hard a voyage had been on supplies and equipment, pirates found treasure in another ship's food and water supplies and extra sailcloth. Desperate pirates were little more than scavengers, practically stripping a ship bare as a list of items stolen in a 1717 raid clearly shows: "needles, twine, kettle, frying pan," while another raid five years later lists: "fourteen boxes of candles, and two boxes of soap." Calico Jack Rackham looted a boat in the West Indies, making a dismal haul of only "50 Rolls of Tobacco, and Nine Bags of Pimiento." A far cry from dreams of gold.

Many pirates claimed to bury their treasure, but little has ever been found. Pirates were known to immediately drink or gamble away their wealth. It is more likely that found treasure belonged to merchants and churches attempting to hide potential "pirate booty."

Pirates often kept ships captured in good condition for their own use. They modified these stolen ships called prizes to suit a raiding lifestyle and to give protection to the main pirate ship.

The Pirate Round

Pirates' ships sailed the Seven Seas following the trade routes of merchant ships in pursuit of treasure for plundering. The rogues' sailing route was known as the Pirate Round. Pirate ships left from Colonial American or Caribbean ports through the Spanish Main off South America, crossing to African coasts, the Indian Ocean, and the Arabian Sea. There they came to the Pirate Coast, at the entrance to the Persian Gulf, and could venture farther into the South China Sea and past the northern tip of Australia. Then it was back over the oceans to their starting port, a voyage that could take them several years.

Pirate Haunts / Nest of Pyrates

All along the Pirate Round, sea rovers found safe haven in ports that tolerated their crude and wild behavior. Popular haunts included Port Royal, Jamaica, the island of Madagascar, and New Providence in the Bahamas, which some labelled the "nest of pyrates." These thrived on the business of piracy – buying stolen goods from the rogues and supplying them with all manner of services, food, and drink during their stay on land. In New Providence, the widow of a sail-maker stitched Jolly Rogers and black jacks for pirate captains. She was paid in whiskey.

Pirates were big spenders and some of the captains had reputations as flamboyant dressers garbed in crimson waistcoats and breeches, silk sashes, and gold chains. But most pirates were a hard and vulgar lot. A clergyman new to the pirate haven of Port Royal, Jamaica was appalled by the presence of "some of the vilest persons in the whole of the world." Another official noted: "All these parts swarm with pirates."

"From the seas"

"From the seas" was the common reply shouted over the waters when a pirate ship was hailed by a passing vessel inquiring as to its origin. The answer was, for the most part, an honest one, for pirate crews were made up of men from whatever port or captured ship they happened to join the band and many had spent a good deal of their lives on the ocean.

No Quarter

"No quarter" meant there would be no mercy shown. If pirates warned a ship to surrender and it showed resistance, or fought back, then the pirates moved in determined to spare not a soul in the ensuing fight. "No quarter shown, no quarter expected in return" was how the pirates saw battle.

Mock Trial

If caught, a pirate was sent to jail, tried for piracy and, most of the time, hanged. Few arrested pirates were found not guilty, or given pardon. With the gruesome image of the gallows ever present in many a pirate's mind, they devised a game to lighten the vision and perhaps even prepare for the inevitability. The pirate mock trial was presented as a kind of a pantomime, with crewmen taking the roles of jailer, hangman, lawyer, and judge. In one instance the acting was so credible, the convicted pirate believed himself condemned to hang. He threw a grenade at the jury and pulled out his cutlass to hack off the prosecutor's arm. He then had to answer in a real pirate trial.

Dancing the Hempen Jig

The standard punishment for a person convicted of piracy was execution by hanging. The hangman's noose was made of hemp, and pirates joked that swinging for their crimes was like doing a dance of death. They referred to hanging as "dancing the hempen jig." When pirates were executed in England, or a British colony, they were hanged at the low-tide mark. It was common practice for their bodies to be hung in gibbet cages – iron body cages made to measure before death by local blacksmiths. The swinging corpses rotted but their bones stayed intact. The grisly display was intended as a public warning that piracy would not be tolerated.

BLACKBEARD

Oh! 'tis of that bloody Blackbeard
I'm going now for to tell;
And as how by gallant Maynard
He soon was sent to hell.

– Attributed to Benjamin Franklin

A TALL AND BURLY WILD-EYED MAN, WITH A thick head of black hair and a long untrimmed beard that hung to his waist and almost covered his face, that was Pirate Captain Edward Teach, alias Blackbeard. His presence was imposing enough for height and hairiness alone, but Blackbeard knew how to build his image to one of devilish proportion.

When Blackbeard lead an attack, he dressed for the occasion. He wore all black, with a wide belt around his waist holding his swords, daggers, and loaded pistols. A bandolier across his chest with six loaded pistols completed his frightening ensemble. His beard and hair were braided into long strands, then twisted, with some plaits pulled up and around his ears and under his hat. Ever the showman, Blackbeard tied red ribbons throughout his beard and wove gunners' matches throughout his hair. The fuses were made of hemp dipped in saltpeter and limewater to make them burn slowly. Just before an attack, Blackbeard would light the matches. He was surely a terrifying spectacle when he jumped on a ship's deck, pistols and swords in hand and smoke coming out from his head in every direction as the fuses smoldered.

Rumors and stories spread of this creature from hell: the demonic captain could cut a man in two with one stroke of his cutlass; he had twelve wives and made each one dance on her wedding night by shooting pistols at her feet; he drank his rum mixed with gunpowder. It was hard to separate the man from the myth, but one Blackbeard tale that circulated was supposedly true and unadorned.

One night, filled with drunken inspiration, Blackbeard stood up among his crew shouting: "We must make a hell of our own and see how long we can bear it." At that he headed straight for the hold, with two or three of the bravest or drunkest following behind him. The group sat themselves down on the stones used as ballast, at which point Blackbeard shouted up an order for some pots filled with brimstone to be brought to them. When the pots were fetched, Blackbeard bolted the hatches and set the brimstone on fire. Suffocating and toxic sulphurous fumes began to fill the hold and the men started to panic, begging to be freed. Blackbeard did not budge until they were all gasping for breath. Only then did he open the hatches and allow his crewmen leave of the hellhole. Blackbeard boasted that he was the one who held out the longest.

In another drunken fit, Blackbeard fired a random shot, shooting a crew member in the knee and making him lame. Asked what made him do it, the captain supposedly answered that if he did not shoot a man now and again, folk would forget who Blackbeard was.

Blackbeard was becoming a terror to all. In an incident off North Carolina, he held several townspeople hostage until his demands for medical supplies were met. To add insult to injury, Blackbeard's band looted the town before leaving. These exploits, as well as rumors that Blackbeard wanted to turn North Carolina's Ocracoke Inlet area into a pirate haven, brought retaliation. Backed by the governor of Virginia, two small sloops were sent into the waters of Ocracoke Inlet, Blackbeard's haunt. Lieutenant Robert Maynard of the Royal Navy was in charge of the attack.

They neared Blackbeard's ship, the *Queen Anne's Revenge*, near nightfall and anchored. Blackbeard, who was partying, looked out to see the sloops and figuring them not to be navy ships, continued his drinking. From time to time, the story goes, Blackbeard looked out at the sloops, then frustrated that he could make nothing out in the dark, mumbled, "O crow cock, O crow cock," which was how Ocracoke supposedly got its name.

By morning light, Maynard led the two sloops toward the *Queen Anne's Revenge*. Blackbeard was quickly on the move in hopes of leading the sloops through narrow channels, where they would run aground. But one of the sloops, the *Ranger*, got too close for the wild captain's comfort and Blackbeard fired his ten guns at it. Six men were killed and ten wounded in the shower of deadly splinters from the impact of the blast.

Maynard and the crew of the second sloop, the *Jane*, used the confusion and smoke to their advantage. Maynard ordered most of his men to hide below deck. When the smoke cleared, Blackbeard looked over at the *Jane* with glee. With so few crewmen aboard, the sloop would be an easy prize. He lashed the two ships together with a rope and his crew made their way aboard. They were soon met by men coming up from every direction and opening leading up to deck. Although Blackbeard's men were greatly outnumbered, still the captain fought with hellish determination.

Face-to-face, Maynard and Blackbeard both fired their pistols at point-blank range. Maynard's shot hit the pirate captain, but Blackbeard continued as before. The two fought, exchanging pistol shot and swinging their swords. The wounded pirate fought furiously and, with a clang, knocked Maynard's sword out of his hand. As Blackbeard moved in for the kill, one of Maynard's men came from behind with a knife and slashed the pirate's throat. Blackbeard reportedly looked over at the young seaman with the knife to tell him, "Well done, lad." The seaman then replied, "If it be not well done, I'll do it better." At that he made another stroke, this time cutting off Blackbeard's head.

Maynard examined the body to discover twenty-five wounds – five made by pistol shot and twenty with blades. Maynard tied the head on a rope and, hanging it like a trophy from the bowsprit, made way his back to Virginia.

Before leaving Ocracoke, Maynard threw Blackbeard's body into the sea and crewmen swore the headless corpse swam three times around the sloop. Still today folk report sightings of the headless pirate swimming through the waters of Ocracoke Inlet.

CUTTHROAT LASSES

ANNE BONNEY AND MARY READ SAILED WITH Calico Jack Rackham. When Anne Bonney met Calico Jack, she ran away with him to be a pirate. They married and worked together aboard the *Vanity*, raiding along the American coast. Disguised as a man, Mary Read had worked on a Dutch ship captured by Rackham. The two women became fast friends and carried on their ruse of dressing as men.

They could swing swords and axes, and fire pistols as well or better than any man pirate. They were fearless fighters and, when Calico Jack's ship was attacked by a man-of-war, Bonney and Read fought the attackers together. They were arrested and tried for piracy in Jamaica. According to testimony given at their trials, the duo could cuss, swear, and be every bit as vicious and threatening as any man. Convicted and sentenced to hang, the two pirates "pleaded their bellies," meaning they were pregnant and by law their lives would be spared. Mary Read died in prison and it is thought Anne Bonney was given her freedom to live a quieter life somewhere in the Caribbean.

THE BALLAD OF CAPTAIN KIDD

The hanging of Captain William Kidd was a gruesome spectacle for those gathered at London's Execution Dock on the Thames River. At low tide Kidd was hanged, but the rope broke. He fell and had to mount the scaffolding a second time. This next try left him dangling and his corpse hung there for the passing of three tides. Captain Kidd's body was then taken down, coated with tar, and fitted in an iron cage called a gibbet. It was hung up once more.

My name was William Kidd, when I sailed, when I sailed,
My name was William Kidd, when I sailed,
My name was William Kidd; God's laws I did forbid,
And so wickedly I did, when I sailed.

My parents taught me well to shun the gates of hell,
But against them I rebelled, when I sailed.

I'd a Bible in my hand, by my father's great command,
And I sunk it in the sand, when I sailed.

I roam'd from sound to sound, and many a ship I found
And them I sunk or burned, when I sailed.

I murdered William Moore and laid him in his gore,
Not many leagues from shore, as I sailed.

I was sick and nigh to death, and I vowed with every breath,
To walk in wisdom's ways, when I sailed.

I thought I was undone, and my wicked glass had run,
But health did soon return, as I sailed.

My repentance lasted not, my vows I soon forgot,
Damnation was my lot, as I sailed.

I spied three ships from France, to them I did advance
And took them all by chance, as I sailed.

I spied three ships from Spain, I looted them for gain,
Till most of them were slain, as I sailed.

I'd ninety bars of gold, and doubloons manifold,
With riches uncontrolled, as I sailed.

Thus being o'ertaken at last, and into prison cast,
And sentence being passed, I must die.

Farewell, the raging main, to Turkey, France, and Spain,
I shall ne'er see you again, for I must die.

Farewell to Lunnon town, the pretty girls all round,
You're welcome to my gold, for I must die.

Now to Execution Dock, I must go, while many
    thousands flock,
But I must bear the shock, and must die.

So it's up a rope I go, with my friends all down below
Say Bill we told you so, I must die.

Come all ye young and old, you're welcome to my gold,
For by it I've lost my soul, and I must die.

Take a warning now by me, and shun bad company,
Lest you come to hell with me, for I must die.

Farewell, the raging main, I must die, I must die
Farewell, the raging main, I must die,
Farewell, the raging main, to Turkey, France, and Spain,
I shall ne'er see you again, for I must die.

WATERY GRAVES

Flame of the Sea

Wild Norse sea pirates manned long and narrow serpent-shaped Viking boats and travelled the northern seas, pillaging and plundering all that crossed their paths. As fearless and bloody as these Norse seafarers could be, they were held in the grips of strong superstitious fears. "Surely," they thought, "the gods and goddesses of such unforgiving waters must be fierce and heartless." The Norse sea rovers carved protective words or verses in magical symbols into the ship's prow – sea runes to calm the waters.

THE NORSE BELIEVED IN TERRIFYING UNDERwater giants who surfaced just to seize hold of a passing Viking ship and spill its crew into the icy waters. Aegir, one of the giants of the deep, was a wild old man whose icy face was framed with white sea-foam hair and who had terrible clawing fingers. When the sea raged, the Vikings believed it was Aegir brewing his mighty kettle until the water bubbled and churned. The grisly Viking rule of sacrifice was to drown every tenth man among their prisoners to appease the tempestuous Aegir, his wretched wife Ran, and their nine daughters – the waves or billow maidens.

Ran, whose very name meant "robber" and "ravisher," was callous and murderous. On a bloodthirsty whim, she stirred up the waters and called up rough winds. Then Ran rose up out of the ocean with her drowning net. Towering over a passing Viking ship (for she was the daughter of a giant), Ran took aim and cast her net over top of the ship's masts and sails. Sailors caught in her net were hauled across the deck and drowned.

Ran dragged each day's catch to the sea god's hall, the *Flame of the Sea*, deep below the waves. The whole palace glimmered with the gold gathered from shipwrecks and drowned men. Sailors carried gold coins, for if they did get caught up and drown in Ran's net – faring to Ran, as it was called – they wanted to be treated to the best in the watery afterlife.

Let none go empty-handed
Down to azure Ran.
Icy are her kisses
Fickle her embraces.
But we'll charm the sea-bride
With our ruddy gold.
　　　　　　　– From "Frithjof's Saga" by Esias Tegnér

Davy Jones' Locker

What the sea wants, the sea will have.

For a mariner of any sort, death on the water seemed to lurk, ever waiting, in the fog banks or just beyond the horizon. Those that met a watery grave by drowning, or from other misfortune, were said to go down to the very bottom of the ocean. There, a giant sea chest waited with open lid to catch and hold the dead. Sailors called the undersea coffin Davy Jones' Locker. Davy Jones, himself, was a dismal and malicious spirit dwelling in the murky depths, ever alert to passing ships above.

Sometimes, so sailors believed, Davy Jones brought on tempests just to capture more souls for his chest. He was even thought to rise at times and drag someone who fell overboard down to his death locker. Many a pirate wore a gold earring to protect himself from drowning, and it was not uncommon for a boat to sail with an iron horseshoe secured under the deck. There were some who would not rescue a drowning man, even one of their own crew, fearing Davy Jones would be cheated of one soul and go swiftly and viciously in search of another.

Most importantly, sailors who feared the demons of the deep would not speak of the devil by name. In fact, some think the name Davy Jones came from sailors trying to avoid saying the devil's name aboard ship – calling him instead Taffy, the thief, and Jonah or Jonas (for the unfortunate man who fell into the belly of a whale). Taffy Jonas became Davy Jones. Others thought the name came from Indian sailors who called their Hindu death goddess Deva Lokka. Gradually the term "Davy Jones" became a taboo that no sailor would dare speak aboard ship.

I'll be damned if it was not Davy Jones himself. I know him by his saucer eyes, his three rows of teeth, and tail, and the blue smoke that came out his nostrils. This same Davy Jones, according to the mythology of sailors, is the fiend that presides over all other evil spirits of the deep, and is often seen in various shapes, perching among the rigging on the eve of hurricanes, shipwrecks, and other disasters to which seafaring life is exposed, warning the devoted wretch of death and woe.

– A fictional rendering of Davy Jones
by novelist Tobias Smollet, 1751

VI

HAUNTING
REFRAINS:
ONLY THE FOG?

WATER WRAITHS

'Twas one dark night I speak of, we were off the shore
  aways;
I never shall forget it in all my mortal days.
'Twas in the dim dark watches I felt a chilling dread;
It bowled me o'er as if I heard one calling from the
  dead.
– From "The Ghostly Sailors," a Newfoundland folk song

ONE OF THE MOST FEARFUL SEA SPECTERS FOR a sailor to witness was the appearance of a water wraith, or ghost, on the open ocean. Many are the accounts that come from sailors working on the late-night watches. Their stories are chilling, for all tell of pale figures of men that rose up from the ocean, hovered over the waves, then began to climb up the sides of a vessel. They were ghoulish and haggard sights, for their faces were a pasty whitish gray and their limbs, long and bony. Their clothes hung all about them – little more than torn rags. They dripped water as they moved about deck. Not one of the wraiths uttered a word and they set about their tasks in eerie silence. The regular crew on watch could only move out of their way. It was apparent by the cold vacant stares of these water wraiths that they noticed no one else aboard.

Meticulously they began their work, laboring in a supernatural rhythm as if hearing a ghostly chantey inaudible to human ears. The dripping wet ghost crew hauled in empty nets, tugging at them as if they held large catches. A ghost captain sat ominously at the helm and piloted the ship. The ghost crew was determined and deliberate in every move as if it was all it knew how to do. All the long night, while the casting and hauling continued, the regular crew was too petrified to interrupt the ghosts. With the day's first light, the water wraiths dropped their work and, with the same grim and silent determination, walked over to the ship's railing and jumped into the sea. When the regular crew looked over, there was not a body to be seen. The ghost crew had returned to the depths, waiting to appear aboard the next ship that sailed at midnight over the very spot where they had met their deaths aboard their own ship.

Seeing a water ghost of a sailor who had drowned, or been killed on the ocean, was believed to be an ill omen for the person to whom it appeared. If a water wraith came out of nowhere and was seen clinging on to the yardarms, it was a sign that the sea was demanding another victim.

But the water wraith that appeared off Sable Island, off Nova Scotia's shores, was not threatening to sailors. In fact, he often gave a helping hand. So many ships have been wrecked off Sable Island, folk call the island the Graveyard of the Atlantic. The wraith of those cruel waters appeared to the crew of one of the lifeboats that performed rescue missions there.

Rowing to a ship in distress, the lifeboat crew noticed what seemed to be a man swimming in the water beyond them. Thinking him a victim of the wrecked vessel, they rowed toward the figure. When they looked down at the water, they were met by the empty glare of deep-set eyes in a deathly white face. The man had a bloody gash on one cheek. Without a sound or change of expression, the man climbed aboard, taking a place with the other rowers. Dripping wet, he grabbed an oar and joined in the rhythm, for no one in the lifeboat dared stop and question what was happening. During the rescue, the man sat in place, staring in a trance out over the ocean. When the lifeboat was ready to return, the wraith picked up the oars in his thin white hands and began rowing back to Sable Island. At the exact spot on the waters where the ghostly rower had first been seen swimming, the wraith dropped his oars, stood up in the boat, and dived over the side, disappearing into the sea.

Many believe the Sable Island water wraith to be the ghost of one of the lifeboat crewmen who had drowned on a dangerous rescue mission. Others believe the mystery was solved by a note found on the island. When the island lighthouse burned down, a man cleaning up the site found a small metal box buried under the heaps of ashes and burnt timber. He opened up the old box and found the Lighthouse Log. One of the recorded entries is thought to clearly identify the helpful specter of Sable Island. The entry read:

> Friday, September 10th, 1826. Stormy Wednesday, blowing South East. No vessels spoken. Howard Murray is dead. He died at ten o'clock this morning. The gash in his right cheek festered and blood poisoning set in. Before he died he said he would come back; that he would always go out in the lifeboat in which he had rowed stroke for twenty-five years. I wonder if he will. We buried him this afternoon on the point.

THE FLYING DUTCHMAN

For centuries the most dreaded sight for mariners sailing around the Cape of Good Hope has been a ghost ship that blazes through the water, with a demonic captain and his ghastly crew of skeletons. Many a sailor has sworn that, without any warning sound or prior sighting on the horizon, a huge vessel appears shrouded in fog, with its full sails beating in the wind, driving it directly into the path of their ship. At the moment that collision seems an inevitability, the vessel vanishes as instantly as it had appeared.

SEVERAL HUNDRED YEARS AGO, A FLAMBOYANT and foul-tempered sea captain from the Netherlands set sail for the East Indies. The Dutch captain's name was Hendrik Vander Decker, his surname meaning "the cloaked one." He had a nasty reputation on the waters, for being driven by greed, he often forced passage through the most turbulent seas and made passengers endure arduous routes. He cared for no one's safety or comfort, but only for making good time and a great deal of money.

On one particular stormy passage, the captain could make little headway as he tried to round the Cape of Good Hope. Before he left port, he had boasted he would make the difficult passage so many had failed at or had died in trying. But as he sailed through the waters off the cape, gale force winds blew in. The passengers panicked and he ordered them to go belowdecks, then locked them there while he sailed onward. His crew was fearful, but when one man protested and tried to restrain the captain, Vander Decker shoved him overboard, where he met his death in stormy seas. The captain laughed maniacally over the howling gales. He boasted once more that he would never stop his attempt to round the cape – that he'd be damned if he would give up, no matter how long it might take.

Vander Decker yelled wicked and defiant words into the winds and up at the heavens. Some say it was then he made a pact with the devil, but others say that the angry captain mocked and jeered the power of nature and swore an unholy and blasphemous oath straight up to God. He vowed that neither God nor devil would prevent him from rounding the "Cape of Storms."

Immediately a misty form descended through the fog, materializing on the quarterdeck as a huge and ghastly figure. Some say it was the devil himself, as the clouds that wreak havoc around the cape are called the Devil's Tablecloth. But most believe it was a divine form, perhaps even the Holy Ghost himself.

Annoyed at the intrusion on his ship, Vander Decker took aim with his pistol and fired. The bullet made no wound on the misty spirit, but deflected and shot through the captain's own hand. Screaming with pain and rage, the Dutchman shook his fist at the presence, then gasped in horror as his whole arm was immediately paralyzed and fell limply to his side.

Whatever the spirit's identity was, it was all-powerful. Chaos was at work all around the Dutchman. Masts snapped in half in the screaming wind. The presence then spoke in a deep and ominous voice, louder than any wind or raging sea:

Vander Decker, you have defied the powers of nature and the sea, and you have cursed me. For this you shall be punished. Forever you shall sail these stormy seas, with never a port for rest or refuge and never good weather. From this moment on, you shall be ever on watch. Should your eyes but droop or try to close for sleep, the pain of a piercing sword and a thousand grains of sand shall make them open to keep vigil on the stormy sea. Endless storms will follow your course and the sight of your ship will bring severe misfortune to all unlucky enough to behold it. For an eternity, I decree you shall be thus cursed.

The wind blew its fury out and Vander Decker realized the presence had left. Relieved the ordeal was over and convinced it was a dream from exhaustion, the captain breathed a deep sigh. But when he gazed around his ship, he was horrified. His whole crew lay about his feet, all of them dead men. Then before his astonished eyes, each corpse turned into a skeleton, rose to salute him, and began work again. Immediately a strong gust blew and rain pelted the deck. In a wild storm, the captain gave the only order he could – to sail for all they were worth.

And from that day forward, the Dutchman wanders the seas. A demon cabin boy remains by his side, not for comfort, but for torment. The hungry captain is served only hot molten iron and cups of gall. His crew expands with the passing of time, made up of every murderous pirate, cowardly or sinning sailor. *The Flying Dutchman*, its captain, and company of the dead are condemned for an eternity to sail without even once dropping anchor.

The demon ship, travelling with storms in its wake, bodes disaster for all who spy it. The captain sends tempests and should he appear on another's ship, wine instantly sours and all food aboard becomes beans. He tries to get sailors to carry his letters to port, but they must never take them or they, too, are dead men. The once boastful captain is a sad and fearful specter, forever sailing his demon ship through bitter winds and storms.

GHOSTLY SEA TALES

As far as I can remember, my father saw what he he said looked like a blazing ship way out on the water. He was walking along the bay shore with several friends and they all saw this vessel on fire at the head of the bay. Dad said there seemed to be figures running around the deck. Then, in an instant, the ship disappeared without so much as a sound.

Another time he was at the steering wheel on midnight watch off Sable Island, the Graveyard of the Atlantic as they called it. All of a sudden he saw something glowing out ahead of him in the water. He said it looked to be a white hand rising out of the sea holding a flaming torch.

What adds some weight to these stories for me is that my father was a seaman who'd been fishing for over forty years. He wasn't a man who was easily fooled by anything.

– *Gordon Mason, Lunenburg, Nova Scotia*

WITCHES' WIND KNOTS

Second Witch: I'll give thee a wind.
Third Witch: And I another.
First Witch: I, myself have all the other;
    And the very ports they blow,
    All the quarters that they know
    I' the shipman's card.

– From *Macbeth*, Act I, Scene III

THE WAY OF THE WIND WAS ALWAYS ON A sailor's mind, and often his life and the success of a voyage was seen to be at the mercy of the wind. A favorable wind brought smooth sailing: no winds at all meant days of becalming, loss of money, dwindling food supplies, heat, and falling prey to pirates and sea beasts. Storm winds brought death and destruction and shipwreck.

Sailors bargained for winds, carrying charms and amulets, and held many superstitions to guarantee fair winds. To sweep in a good and steady wind, sailors often nailed brooms fast to the mainmast. Some scratched on the mast, or whistled when they wanted a breeze, and sailors from the Scottish Hebrides were known to fasten the skin of a male goat to the masthead to attract a good wind.

Some sailors actually paid money to insure good wind and fortune. Before leaving on a long voyage, they went to see women who were regarded as witches. Sometimes the sailors would have their fortunes, and their vessel's fortune, told. But mostly they went to buy favorable winds.

Many were wary of witches, believing them to cast strange spells over the elements by tossing stones, boiling hog bristles, or sprinkling water in the air in curious patterns. They believed these witches had the power to brew mists, stir up tempests, bring hail, and level bolts of lightning at ships at sea. Still there were some witches who were willing to share their secrets, sparing sailors their wrath as long as an exchange of money was made.

Witches sold wind to seamen in the form of a knotted cord. And the secret of how to use the three wind knots on the cord was shared with the purchaser. A mariner stranded in a becalmed sea could call in the amount of wind necessary to keep on course. Untying the first knot, a jaunty breeze would begin. Untying the second knot brought the stronger winds of a gale, and untying the third guaranteed a tempest of hurricane proportions.

He undid the first knot, and there blew a fine breeze. On opening the second, the breeze became a gale. On nearing the Irish shore, he loosed the third, and such a hurricane arose that some of the houses on shore were destroyed. On coming back to Kintyre, he was careful to loose only two knots on the remaining string.

– Account of John McTaggart's voyage
between Kintyre and Ireland, recorded 1870

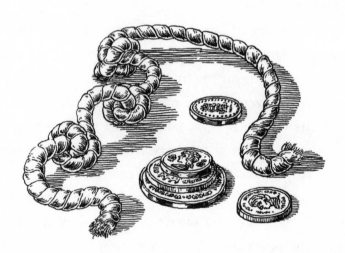

GHOSTLY SUPERSTITIONS

Evil Portents:

- Eclipses of the sun and moon are considered evil omens.
- An Icelandic belief is that a crescent moon, with its horns turned down toward the earth, means shipwreck within the phases of that moon.
- The aurora borealis is a sign of an approaching tempest.
- If rats leave a ship in harbor, that ship will be lost at sea. Rats leave instinctively, knowing they will not be dry aboard.
- The ninth wave is called the avenging or death wave. This wave is thought to be vicious and destructive and only by making the sign of the cross above it can it be rendered powerless.

Sea Witches:

- A sailor who thinks he is under the evil spell of a witch can find protection from her interference by touching cold iron.

- Iron controls the water demons and fiends.
- One Cornish tale is about a rock called the Ness. Should a sailor land there, he will be sought by angry waves unless he throws all iron in his possession into the sea.
- Another tale from the Cornish coast tells of the Fraddam witch, who floats in a tub using a broomstick for an oar. Any sailor who spies the witch will be drowned soon afterward. Sailors and coastal people break the shells of eggs after they have eaten the insides to prevent witches from using the shells as boats.

Demons:

- The story goes that a smuggler coming up the Cornish coast could not, no matter how hard he tried, make port. He curses and tears his hair out, throwing it to the winds to appease the source of his woe, the storm-raising demon.
- Guernsey sailors who see the hideous dwarf goblin, Jochinus, will soon meet death by drowning. Jochinus is said to be a greenish sea monster, with sharp claws and long fins for feet. He calls out the names of the drowned, and knows where all make their watery graves.
- On dark nights, the east wind is thought to be caused by curlews – birds that many sailors believe have direct dealings with storm-demons and spirits. To spot curlews in flight means severe storms, and sailors call the birds the seven whistlers. Their old saying was: "When seabirds fly to land, a storm is at hand."

Charms:

- In Scotland, at the time of the Middle Ages, sailors carried a stone on which they engraved a ship. The special stone guarded against shipwreck.
- Sailors wear a belt of seaweed tied in magic knots as a protective charm at sea.
- A pebble thrown up on deck by the sea is considered a lucky charm.

Death:

- If the body of a drowned man washes up on a Scottish beach, many seamen will not touch it, believing that to do so means they will end up meeting the same fate.
- Scottish sailors refuse to sail aboard boats where others have been drowned.
- In the Middle Ages, a common belief was that the needle of the compass would not move should there be a dead body aboard the boat.
- Deaths occur at the ebb of a tide.

VII

SEA CHANTEYS:
SALTY DOGS

THE SAILORS' ALPHABET

The song of a sailor is called a chantey. It most probably derived from the French verb chanter, *which means "to sing." Often sailors sang rhythmic chanteys to help their work along, so chanteys came to be categorized by the workstation onboard ship. Sailors raising or lowering the anchor sang capstan chanteys; those hauling sheets or fastening the bowline sang popular short-drag chanteys like "Haul Away Joe." "The Sailors' Alphabet" is a forecastle chantey. The forecastle is the forward section of a vessel where sailors lived when they were not working. Because the forecastle was a place to relax and sleep, the chanteys sung in the forecastle were not about work, but were full of fun and tall tales. Like other chanteys, no one knows who started the singing of "The Sailors' Alphabet." All that is known is that it was first heard in the forecastles of boats sometime in the 1800s.*

Oh, A is the anchor and that you all know,
B is the bowsprit that's over the bow,
C is the capstan with which we heave round,
And D are the decks where our sailors are found.
Oh, E is the ensign our mizzen peak flew,
F is the fo'c'sle where we muster our crew,
G are the guns, sir, by which we all stand,
And H are the halyards that ofttimes are manned.
Oh, I is the iron of our stunsail boom sheet,
J is the jib that weathers the bleat,
K is the keelson away down below,
And L are the lanyards that give us good hold.
M is our mainmast so stout and so strong,
N is the needle that never points wrong,
O are the oars of our jolly boat's crew,
And P is the pennant of red, white, and blue.
Q is the quarterdeck where our captain oft stood,
R is the rigging that ever holds good,
S are the stilliards that weigh out our beef,
And T are the topsails we ofttimes do reef.
Oh, U is the Union at which none dare laugh,
V are the vangs that steady the gaff,
W's the wheel that we all take in time,
And X is the letter for which we've no rhyme.
Oh, Y are the yards that we ofttimes do brace,
Z is the letter for which we've no place,

The bosun pipes grog, so we'll all go below,
My song it is finished, I'm glad that it's so.

A song is as good as ten men.
           – Sailors' saying

STRIKE THE BELL

Time aboard ship was kept by the striking of the ship's bell once for every half hour that passed in a watch. On North American and English vessels, four-hour watches divided the workday. One of the four-hour watches was divided again to make two dogwatches.

The Watches:

12:00 noon to 4:00 p.m. – afternoon watch

4:00 p.m. to 6:00 p.m. – first dogwatch

6:00 p.m. to 8:00 p.m. – second dogwatch

8:00 p.m. to 12:00 mid. – first watch

12:00 mid. to 4:00 a.m. – middle or churchyard watch

4:00 a.m. to 8:00 a.m. – morning watch

8:00 a.m. to 12:00 noon – forenoon watch

The crew of the ship is itself divided into two watches. The larboard (or larbord) watch is the port (left side) watch and is commanded by the first mate. The other watch is the starboard (right side) watch.

Eight bells would at last be struck, and the men on deck, exhilarated by the prospect of changing places with us, would call the watch in a most provokingly mirthful and facetious style.

As thus: Larbord watch, ahoy! eight bells there, below! Tumble up, my lively hearties . . .

– From *Redburn* by Herman Melville

SALTY DOG TALK

When sailors use the following expressions, here is what they really mean:

Bone in her teeth – foam of the bow waves
Mug-up – a hot drink and a small snack
Merry men of May – currents created by an ebbing tide
No more cats than can catch mice – a crew barely large enough to handle the necessary work on ship – no extra hands
Up-and-down wind – no wind blowing
Mudhook – anchor
Hurrah's nest – complete confusion
Herring choker – fisherman
Crinkum Crankum – whale too clever to be caught
Cape Horn snorter – heavy gale
Cut one's painter – to die or to leave ship

Bluenoser – Nova Scotian

Blue-water man – deep-sea mariner

Deep six – the deep sea. When an object is thrown overboard and sinks, it has been given the deep six.

In everybody's mess and nobody's watch – said of an idle sailor or a busybody

Tom Pepper – a terrific liar

Stem to stern – from one end to the other

Scuttlebutt – gossip

Shipshape – everything aboard is in good condition and in place

Glass has fell – sandglass that measures time and marks the end of a watch, or the barometer, which is either rising or falling

Aft at the wheel – steering wheel at the stern of a ship

Glasses in his hand – telescope in his hand

Shortening sail – taking in the sail so the vessel will reduce speed

SAILORS' SUPERSTITIONS

Winds, Weather, and Storm:

Never a circle to the moon
Should send your topmasts down,
But when it is around the sun,
With all the masts it must be done.

— Breton proverb

- Shooting stars mean a tempest is in the offing.
- If a sailor hears a child crying in a woman's arms, there will be a storm when he goes to sea.
- If a sailor violates a sworn oath, there will be a storm.
- If a sailor plots a nasty act, he will sail through a storm.
- A sailor who cuts his hair or nails during a calm will provoke a gale. Hair and nails should be cut only in a storm.

- Some boatmen in India kept venomous snakes in their boats. If, while docked in harbor, the snakes were dull, the boat stayed put; only a lively snake was thought to foretell a lucky voyage.
- Playing a game of cards can provoke a storm.
- Throwing a burning coal overboard brings a storm.
- Sailors will not sew or mend any item when the wind is contrary, for they believe they would be sewing up the wind.
- To speak of the wind when it is good is asking for trouble. It will change upon speaking.
- There are some inventive ways used to "call up the wind": the sounds of certain musical instruments can bring on winds, or sometimes even storms. Chinese sailors beat tom-toms and crashed cymbals together to summon a favorable wind. Ancient French mariners flogged a cabin boy at the mast to whip up a wind.

Lucky and Unlucky:

> *On a Friday she was launched,*
> *On a Friday she set sail,*
> *On a Friday met a storm,*
> *And was lost too in a gale.*
>
> – Sailor's song

- Certain letters of the alphabet are considered unlucky to use in a ship's name. The letter *S* is an unlucky letter, and ships with

O in their names are more likely to have an unlucky voyage. Some *O* vessels were such unfortunate ventures they suffered burned and completely ruined cargoes.

- Three *A*'s in a vessel's name is lucky.
- Spanish sailors thought it unlucky to place the left foot onshore first, or to step onto a boat left foot first. It was unlucky for a sailor's wife to rest her broom behind the door, with the bristles up, while her husband was at sea.
- It is unlucky to have eggs aboard ship.
- Casting a penny over the bow at the outset of a voyage brings good luck.
- It is unlucky to set out to sea in a direction opposite to the course of the sun.
- An umbrella, whether opened or closed, aboard ship is bad luck.
- To lose a broom or a mop at sea is an unlucky occurrence.
- Not only is it unlucky to lose a water bucket at sea, it's a bad omen to knock over a bucket or upturn it.
- Should a fisherman meet a woman with a white apron, when on his way to his boat, he should turn around and wait a tide.
- Flat-footed people and those with red hair are to be avoided. Should either be encountered, make sure to speak first.
- It is unlucky to throw a stone over the side of a vessel putting to sea, for the vessel will never return.
- The ringing note made by touching the rim of a glass means a shipwreck, unless it is abruptly stopped by putting a finger on the rim.

- The word "drown" is never to be uttered at sea.
- Sailors believe it unlucky to change a vessel's name. Many ships have been wrecked or lost after such a change.
- It is considered unlucky for two relatives to sail together as crew on the same ship. One of them will drown.
- Should a sailor have an itchy nose when he first steps aboard ship, he should turn to starboard to sneeze. A port sneeze is unlucky for the voyage.
- It is bad luck to spit in the hold of a schooner.
- Mentioning the word "pig" onboard a vessel is bad luck. Instead of pig, some sailors speak of Mr. Dennis.
- Vessels in harbor should be docked on the east side of a wharf for luck.
- Gray mittens must never be worn aboard ship.
- While it is bad luck to spill salt, it is lucky for a sailor to carry a pinch of salt in his pocket.
- Lucky sailing days: Sunday, Monday, Wednesday, Thursday. Unlucky sailing days: Tuesday, Friday.
- Saying the word "egg" while aboard ship is taboo. Sailors may call them cackleberries or hen-fruit, if they must refer to eggs at all.
- A coin placed under the masthead of a vessel brings good fortune.

Tides and Waves:
- A child should not make faces when the tide is high for fear his face might be permanently fixed in a grimace.

- Folk along the coast of Brittany believed most babies were born with the incoming tide.
- A sickness often follows the tide – an ill person feels worse when the tide is coming in and better when the tide is going out. Although, another saying goes: "Strength returns with the rising tide."
- If you cut your hair as the tide is rising, you will catch a bad cold.
- It is best to make butter when the tide is coming in.
- Toothache can be cured by seawater drawn from the crest of the third wave.
- Water from the third wave is powerful and can be used to cast spells or ward off evil.
- Prayers for safety should be repeated with every ninth wave.

Charms and Lucky Objects:
- A pig tattooed on a sailor's foot is a charm to prevent drowning.
- The figurehead is the guardian of the ship. Some old mariners believed it protected them from storms, while others thought the eyes of the figurehead could guide the vessel through dangerous seas. They said prayers of gratitude and made offerings of bread and wine to the figurehead to ensure clear sailing.
- Black walnut wood was never used in shipbuilding as some sailors believed it was from the tree of the devil himself and would surely attract a bolt of lightning. Oak and pine were the best woods to use as they did not attract lightning.

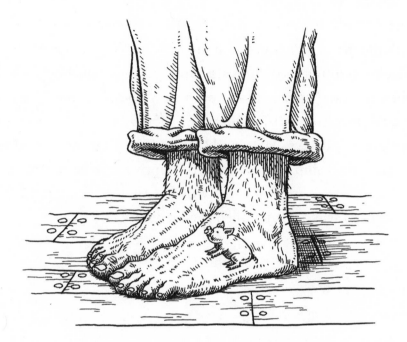

- Eyes are painted on the bow of ships to ward off evil and dark magic.
- A horseshoe nailed to the mainmast is a protection against evil.
- If sailors cross their first and second fingers, ill luck is kept at bay. Some sailors spit into their hats or into the palms of their left hands.
- Blowing a trumpet at a whirlpool can scare it off.
- Some Polynesian and Micronesian sailors keep a piece of brain coral under their seat in the boat. The brain coral represents the sea god whose help is called for to bring about a safe crossing. Little carved figures are also thrown overboard to ensure a safe passage.

- The "ship's Jonah" is any presence aboard a vessel that is thought to be the source of ill fortune. The reference is to Jonah, who was thrown overboard and swallowed by a whale. A 1958 newspaper account blamed a budgie named Joey for the misfortunes of the *Queen Elizabeth*, which encountered nothing but delays, gales, and storms. The disgruntled bird was labelled the "ship's Jonah" and promptly escorted off the liner.
- Sailors break a small piece of wood with a cracking noise as a counter charm. This is called the lucky break.

Sound the conch, Triton
so all who hear may know
the song of the great ocean –
gentle and lulling; harsh and tempestuous.
Always deep with mysteries.
An eternal and forever song.

AUTHOR'S NOTE

The journey of writing *Song of the Sea* has been exciting, full of surprising information at every turn. It became evident to me that the world of folklore and myth is very much alive. A story of mermaid tears I heard in 1976 during a stay in the Scottish Hebrides was told to me some twenty years later on Brier Island, a small island sitting in Nova Scotia's Bay of Fundy. It struck me how wonderful it is that a folktale could travel across the Atlantic Ocean from one remote island location to another, washing up on a new shore.

I first heard many of the stories, songs, and bits of lore in this book around kitchen tables in Lunenburg, Nova Scotia. I heard many more from Newfoundland sea captains and singing cooks. My summers in Scotland and travels throughout New England enhanced my appreciation of the richness, vibrancy, and universality of sea lore.

SOURCES

Bassett, Fletcher S., *Legends and Superstitions of the Sea and of Sailors, in All Lands and at All Times*. Chicago: Belford, Clarke, 1885.

Beck, Horace, *Folklore and the Sea*. Middletown, Conn.: Published for the Marine Historical Association by Wesleyan University Press, 1973.

Benwell, Gwen and Waugh, Arthur, *Sea Enchantress: The Tale of the Mermaid and Her Kin*. New York: The Citadel Press, 1965.

Caswell, Helen, *Shadows from the Singing House: Eskimo Folk Tales*. Rutland, Vermont: Charles E. Tuttle Company, Inc., 1968.

Clark, Ella E., *Indian Legends of the Pacific Northwest*. Berkeley: University of California Press, 1958.

Cordingly, David, *Under the Black Flag: The Romance and the Reality of Life Among the Pirates*. New York: Random House, 1995.

Crossley-Holland, Kevin, *Norse Myths*. Hemel Hempstead: Simon & Schuster Young Books, 1993.

Evslin, Bernard, *Scylla and Charybdis*. New York: Chelsea House Publishers, 1989.

Guerber, H. A., *Myths of Northern Lands*. New York: American Book Company, 1895.

Keary, A. & E., *The Heroes of Asgard*, Children's Edition. London: Macmillan & Co., 1930.

MacKenzie, Donald A., *Wonder Tales From Scottish Myth & Legend*. London: Blackie and Son Limited, 1917.

Malcolmson, Anne and McCormick, Dell J., *Mister Stormalong*. Boston: Houghton Mifflin, Cambridge: The Riverside Press, 1952.

Metaxas, Eric, *Stormalong*. Rowayton, CT: Rabbit Ears Productions, Inc., 1992.

Monaghan, Patricia, *The New Book of Goddesses and Heroines*. 3rd edition, St. Paul, MN: Llewellyn Publications, 1998.

Opie, Iona and Tatem, Moira, *A Dictionary of Superstitions*. Oxford: Oxford University Press, 1989.

Philip, Neil, *Odin's Family*. New York: Orchard Books, 1996.

Shay, Frank, *An American Sailor's Treasury: Sea Songs, Chanteys, Legends, and Lore,* Two Volumes in One. New York: Smithmark Publishers Inc., 1991.

Stone, Merlin, *Ancient Mirrors of Womanhood: Our Goddess and Heroine Heritage*, Volumes I and II. New York: New Sybilline Books, 1979.

Sturluson, Snorri, *The Prose Edda*, translated by Arthur Gilchrist Brodeur, New York: The American-Scandinavian Foundation, 1929.

Thomson, David, *The People of the Sea*. Edinburgh: Canongate Books, 1996.

Waddell, Helen, *The Princess Splendour and other stories*. London: Longmans Young Books Ltd., 1969.